CLASSROOM OF THE ELITE

NOVEL 9

STORY BY

Syougo Kinugasa

ART BY

Tomoseshunsaku

Seven Seas Entertainment

CLASSROOM OF THE ELITE VOL. 9
YOUKOSO JITSURYOKUSHIJOUSHUGI NO KYOUSHITSU E VOL. 9
© Syougo Kinugasa 2018
Art by Tomoseshunsaku
First published in Japan in 2018 by KADOKAWA CORPORATION, Tokyo.
English translation rights arranged with KADOKAWA CORPORATION, Tokyo.

Seven Seas press and purchase enquiries can be sent to
Marketing Manager Lianne Sentar at press@gomanga.com.
Information regarding the distribution and purchase of
digital editions is available from Digital Manager CK Russell
at digital@gomanga.com.

Seven Seas and the Seven Seas logo are trademarks of
Seven Seas Entertainment. All rights reserved.

Follow Seven Seas Entertainment online at
sevenseasentertainment.com.

TRANSLATION: Timothy MacKenzie
COVER DESIGN: Nicky Lim
INTERIOR LAYOUT & DESIGN: Clay Gardner
PROOFREADER: Meg van Huygen, Stephanie Cohen
LIGHT NOVEL EDITOR: Nibedita Sen
PREPRESS TECHNICIAN: Rhiannon Rasmussen-Silverstein
PRODUCTION MANAGER: Lissa Pattillo
MANAGING EDITOR: Julie Davis
ASSOCIATE PUBLISHER: Adam Arnold
PUBLISHER: Jason DeAngelis

ISBN: 978-1-64827-261-5
Printed in Canada
First Printing: September 2021
10 9 8 7 6 5 4 3 2 1

1

ICHINOSE HONAMI'S SOLILOQUY

I've never really thought of myself as a good person, never thought of myself as a bad person. I suppose I've managed to become an honest person, just like my mother would've wanted.

Things were fine in elementary school and in junior high. I had lots of friends, guys and girls—everybody. I had a little trouble handling sports, sure, but I pushed myself just like I did with my studies. By my third year of junior high, I'd managed to become student council president, something I'd always aspired to. I'd even managed to get into a private high school as a scholarship student.

A nice school life.

A nice home life.

But I...I made a mistake.

Something that never should've happened. An unfor-givable "mistake" that I never should've made.

The angry look on my ailing mother's face as she lay sick in bed. Her tears. The look of heartbreak on my little sister's face, hurt and distant as she was, retreating into herself, shutting herself away... I can't ever forget it. It comes to me even now.

My trembling fingers.

My trembling body.

The creeping blackness spreading across my heart.

I tossed my third-year of junior high in the trash. For about half a year, I shut myself away.

But...one day, that all came to an end.

When I learned about this school, I knew I needed to put an end to it. I'd ...bring smiles back to the faces of my mother and little sister again. I wouldn't run away from my own "sin." No, I'd face it head-on.

Or so I swore.

But...

I enrolled in this school with a dream, but an ordeal awaited me. When I found the letter, I completely froze, and all around me, my classmates turned to watch curiously.

I read the letter over and over. But no matter how many times I read it, the words refused to change.

"Ichinose Honami is a criminal."

1.1

●●

Long, long before that incident, she'd been in the student council office on a day when school was off, feeling incredibly nervous.

"Ichinose Honami from first-year, Class B, right?"

"Yes," she managed to squeeze out. Ichinose Honami faced Student Council Vice President Nagumo, her nerves clear on her face.

This was a special one-on-one interview.

"What did the Student Council President say to you?" he asked.

"He said that now still wasn't the time..."

Ichinose had wished to join the student council right from the start. She'd come knocking at their door right after enrolling, but Student Council President Horikita had rejected her request after interviewing her, leaving her dejected. However, Vice President Nagumo reached out to her as soon as he heard what happened.

Why? Three reasons: First, she belonged to Class B, just like him. Second, her grades were excellent. Finally, she was quite attractive, which Nagumo always appreciated from the fairer sex.

And Ichinose easily met that last and most important requirement. The first two reasons were, after all, just icing on the cake. She had aesthetic value to him, which made her a valuable piece of property to be kept by his side.

"I heard that you were on the student council when you were in junior high," said Nagumo. "The president, in fact. Is that right?"

"Yes. That's why I wanted to join the one here." Ichinose told the truth. But also a lie.

"Yes, your homeroom teacher, Hoshinomiya-sensei, told me. It sounds like you had excellent scores on your entrance exam, too," said Nagumo.

"Thank you very much," she said humbly, though she didn't meet Nagumo's eyes.

"You are, honestly, quite exceptional."

"Yes, but...Student Council President Horikita didn't acknowledge any of it," said Ichinose with a bitter smile. Shame nipped at her, shame that she hadn't managed to secure the position she knew she deserved. Even so, that faint hint of a smile remained. She wouldn't be able to make a good impression if she came in here looking all down in the dumps.

"Yes, President Horikita's quite strict. Frankly, he probably passed on you because you weren't placed in Class A. He's a real stickler for position, you see."

"I see," said Ichinose.

Of course, Nagumo was lying.

At first glance, Horikita Manabu *looked* like the sort who would fixate and fuss about position. In truth, he was the very opposite. He looked deep within a person and saw the core of who they were. He knew the exceptional when he witnessed it, whether they were in Class D or Class A. But to Ichinose, still stung by his rejection, what Nagumo said felt like the truth.

Ichinose sighed. "I guess I have no choice but to get to Class A if I want to join the student council."

"I don't know about that. Even if you do make it to Class A, President Horikita may never acknowledge you. The fact is, Ichinose, that you were never considered a thoroughbred from the moment you entered this school. No matter how hard you work from here on, President Horikita will never accept a student who was placed in Class B," said Nagumo.

With one cruel statement, the faint smile on Ichinose's face vanished.

"B-but, you're in Class B, Nagumo-senpai. And you're vice president, so—"

Nagumo immediately dashed whatever faint hopes she had left.

"In my case, there were two reasons. You see, I joined the student council before Horikita-senpai became president. Back then, it was a different third-year student who served as president. Horikita-senpai was the Vice President, and the sole person on the student council to object to my appointment. He fought until the bitter end."

Ichinose's expression grew sadder. Seeing that filled Nagumo's heart with joy. He decided that he definitely needed her on the student council, to toy with as his personal plaything.

"The other thing," he continued, "is that I *know* myself. I know my high potential. Rightfully, I *should* have been placed in Class A. When I expressed my desire to join the student council, I confessed the full truth behind why they'd assigned me to Class B. I told them everything right away."

"Confessed...?"

"Indeed. I had proven that in terms of ability, I wasn't

willing to play second fiddle to Class A. That's what led to my current position."

"Nagumo-senpai," said Ichinose, "what...were those things you confessed?"

Nagumo bit back a smile. "Now, now, Ichinose. Aren't you the one being questioned?"

"M-Me?"

"I'm not quite convinced of something. See...normally, it would've been perfectly reasonable for you to be placed in Class A. Your grades are excellent, and your communication skills are nothing to scoff at. And if you take into account your track record as student council president... well, why would you wind up in Class B? There must be some reason."

Ichinose couldn't hide her embarrassment at his deduction, but this was an inevitable outcome. Nagumo had made his conclusions based on information he'd obtained from Ichinose's homeroom teacher, Hoshinomiya-sensei, ahead of time.

"Tell me," he continued, "here and now, what you think the reason is. If you can convince me that you are a student worthy of Class A, then I shall take responsibility for bringing you onto the student council."

"Is that... possible?"

"President Horikita's authority is absolute, certainly.

But what will happen after Horikita-senpai graduates? If first-years don't join the student council, it will be impossible for us to train future members. Imagine the trouble that would cause for the next student council president—namely, me. Do you understand?"

"I...suppose I do, yes..."

"Someone who can't seize this chance isn't qualified to join the student council."

Ichinose's secret gnawed at her from deep inside. Memories of spending half of her third year of junior high cooped up in her room came rushing back.

"What I say here—"

"Will be confidential. Your secrets are ours to keep, and ours alone."

The past that she'd thought she could live with. The past that she'd thought she could conceal forever. But how could she move forward without trusting others? She'd lost that trust...so maybe confiding in people would help her to trust again. Would help others to trust her.

"...I... I—"

And so, Ichinose told him everything.

She told him about her "mistake."

2 THE STUDENT COUNCIL PRESIDENT'S INCLINATION

EARLY IN FEBRUARY, after our time at the school camp was over, we returned to the Advanced Nurturing High School. First-year Class A student Sakayanagi Arisu was in the student council office. She placed her favorite hat upon the desk and sat face-to-face with Student Council President Nagumo Miyabi, from second-year Class A.

"The student council office looks a little gaudy now, doesn't it? Nothing like how it used to be," said Sakayanagi.

Putting it nicely, she was being sincere. The student council office could previously have been described, at best, as being stuffy and formal. Now even the wallpaper had been changed, and a large number of small items that looked like Nagumo's personal effects had been brought in. Rather than a student council office, it looked like Nagumo's own room.

Which was precisely what Nagumo wanted: to show his authority. Or so Sakayanagi mused.

"Don't tell me that Horikita-senpai encouraged you to join the student council," said Nagumo. Sakayanagi surely didn't have any other business with the council. Why was she here?

"Unfortunately, it seems that I didn't meet his standards," she said. "I wasn't invited to join."

"His mistake."

"Does that mean you're different, Mr. New Student Council President?"

A faint smile crept onto Nagumo's lips. "I am. I would gladly welcome you aboard. Of course, you'd be my personal property, at best." He lightly patted the head of a stuffed rabbit that sat nearby.

Was Nagumo fond of stuffed animals? Maybe a girl who hung around him was?

Personal property, he said. In other words, he didn't care about her talents, but was assessing her on looks alone. Sakayanagi could've pretended not to notice, but... why not press him a little? "What would I have to do for your seal of approval, President Nagumo?"

"Demonstrate an appropriate level of skill for me. You know, it's not too late for you to join us. You could come over to my side, Sakayanagi."

"I could," replied Sakayanagi, smiling broadly. "But I won't. I don't think one organization could support two leaders. More importantly, I couldn't bear the thought of crushing the dignity of the upperclassmen."

"Two leaders, huh?" he repeated. So this first-year thought herself to be Nagumo's equal? Or perhaps even greater?

But Nagumo didn't take the bait, didn't get angry. Far from it: he smiled.

"What interesting first-year students we have this year," he said. "Ryuuen and you are *quite* unique."

Almost nobody at this school would consider making an enemy out of the student council. More than a few students tried to buddy up with them to climb the ranks to Class A. Others would just try to stay out of the council's way. But Sakayanagi and Ryuuen didn't hesitate to bare their fangs at anyone...and they didn't show a shred of mercy.

"I can't really say that's a wise way of living," Nagumo added.

There probably are students who would have some respect for those who made enemies on all sides, but

Nagumo wasn't like that. He esteemed those who were sometimes willing to discard their pride and use their power in order to get ahead in the world.

Nagumo's words hung in the air for a moment before his phone, sitting on a nearby desk, vibrated once. Twice. Thrice—

"Is this a bad time?" asked Sakayanagi.

"No. I choose how I spend my time, and I'm devoting it to you right now. Don't worry about it."

"My, it must be difficult being so very popular. All these incessant messages, hm?"

"If you want to respect my time, why don't we get down to business? You don't want to be appointed to the student council? Fine. So what business do you have with me that requires clearing out the entire room? I have a prior engagement with another first-year after this, so I'd appreciate it if you cut to the point."

"I see. Then I suppose I'll keep this brief, hm?"

Sakayanagi's expression didn't change, even though Nagumo had intentionally mentioned meeting with a "first-year." But despite her appearance, Nagumo was sure he'd piqued her interest.

"I've come here today to ask you for one favor," said Sakayanagi. "It's regarding a member of the student council, Ichinose Honami, from first-year Class B. I will be mounting an attack against her. It's quite possible that things might get...*rough*."

"I'm aware. And?"

Nagumo urged her to continue speaking. Everything Sakayanagi had said so far, she'd already told him in a previous meeting between the two of them. Of course, virtually no one knew that meeting had even taken place.

"She is the sole first-year serving on the student council," Sakayanagi said. "Which makes her a likely candidate for the future student council president."

Nagumo nodded. "As long as no other first-year students come forward to join the student council or no exceptionally talented new faces appear, yes. She's pretty much a shoo-in."

"Yes, I suppose that's true."

In other words, losing Ichinose would be bad for the student council...and for Nagumo.

"As my way of thanking you for the other day, I thought I'd inform you of something in advance. In a worst-case scenario, it is quite possible that Ichinose Honami-san will be expelled. I must ask you to please pardon that," declared Sakayanagi, showing no hint of fearing Nagumo.

"I don't recall ever giving you permission to go *that* far, Sakayanagi."

For the first time since their conversation started, the smile had vanished from Nagumo's face.

"Yes, you told me to stop bullying Ichinose-san, President. However, I was thinking I might play a little rough."

"Ichinose is my personal property, and I plan on, ah, *cherishing* her. I gave you permission to weaken her, no more."

"I'm well aware. But *you* should be aware that things don't always go as planned."

Nagumo stared at Sakayanagi sharply. Some might even call it a glare. But Sakayanagi coolly shook off his gaze.

"So...you won't mind, would you? Even if she does happen to be expelled?"

Nagumo shifted slowly in his chair, moving his elbows from the armrests. "Quite a bold girl. You're not afraid of me, are you?"

"That's just the way I am."

"Tell me one thing. You could have just gone ahead and done this without getting my permission. And yet you came all the way here, dutiful as you are, to ask me? You don't want to make an enemy out of me. Is that right?" asked Nagumo, not remotely buying Sakayanagi's claim that she was doing this to thank him.

"Interpret it however you wish; I do not mind."

"Don't lie to me. I want to hear your honest opinion."

Nagumo didn't need her flattery. He wanted to know her true intentions.

"The student council at this school possesses more power than I'd thought. If the student council..." She paused. "No, *if Student Council President Nagumo* took direct action to protect Ichinose-san, that would be troublesome. Even for me."

Ah. So Sakayanagi didn't want him to protect Ichinose. Nagumo flashed his bright white teeth in a grin, seemingly satisfied. Even though she'd expressed it in an indirect way, she was saying that she didn't want to make Nagumo her enemy.

"Seems like the information I gave you has been useful," he said.

"Yes. Thanks to you, I was able to strike Ichinose-san where she was weakest. I'll be making even more effective use of that information moving forward."

"All right, then," said Nagumo. "The student council will... tolerate everything that you're going to do from here on out."

"When you say that the student council will tolerate my actions, is it safe to assume that includes you?" Sakayanagi hadn't missed the fact that Nagumo had deliberately omitted some words when he made his promise.

"...Heh. Well, there'd be no way for me to back out if I specifically said that I, too, was part of that, as someone on the council. What are you planning to do?"

"You'll just have to look forward to finding out. That's all I'll say."

No, revealing her strategy to Nagumo would do her no good—Sakayanagi was sure of it. The man who sat before her was a weasel. Even now, he was ready to throw one of the student council's major players under the bus.

"By the way," she continued, "I don't have too many opportunities to speak with you one-on-one, so there's something else I'd like to ask you"

"What's that?" asked Nagumo.

"I'm not saying it's likely, but...let's say the situation worsens. Let's say *drastic measures* become necessary. Why, a student might try to resolve things with brute force, President. What do you think of that?"

Sakayanagi knew how to deal with resourceful types like Katsuragi, Ichinose, or Horikita. An act of violence, on the other hand...that would be a problem. Sakayanagi would be helpless against such a thing. She wouldn't stand a chance.

"You're not well-equipped to deal with the kind of person who'd make a last-ditch attempt to overpower their opponent through force, huh?" asked Nagumo.

"It's not my forte." She did suffer from a physical handicap—that couldn't be helped.

"Unfortunately, I don't particularly dislike the use of force, myself. And fighting is entirely unavoidable for us students, don't you think? I have no intention of cracking down on it like Horikita-senpai did. Really, now, why can't we just laugh off a little skirmish now and then?"

Surely this would put Sakayanagi, who couldn't fight, at a bit of a disadvantage...but no, her concerns were about something else entirely.

"Hm. In that case, President Nagumo, I'd like to ask you about an issue from some time ago. The fight that broke out between first-year Class D and Class C. If you'd been in power at the time, would have you handed down a different judgment than the previous student council president?"

The business with Sudou, Ishizaki and his guys. Which side threw punches? And which got beat up? The case had been fought over whether there were security cameras there to pick up what happened. Nagumo hadn't been directly involved in that incident, but he had to know about it, given how closely he always shadowed Horikita Manabu.

"Let's see...well, I wouldn't let the people involved off the hook after they dragged our entire school into their mess, but I don't think I'd go so far as to call for expulsion. I wouldn't push for class points or private points to be docked either. My choice of punishment would be suspension.," said Nagumo. "That is, ah, just my opinion as a representative of the student council."

No matter how tolerant the student council chose to be, the school had the final say in the matter. Sakayanagi probably was fully aware of that fact, too. They might wield significantly more power than your average student council, but they were still students, at the end of the day. They couldn't forget that part.

"I see. How magnanimous of you," said Sakayanagi.

And that magnanimity would just so happen to make intimidation and violence a school-wide reality in the future. Sakayanagi would have to take that into account.

"If you're feeling uneasy about that, I can always get some second-years to accompany you."

In other words, the second-years in question would overwhelm the first-years by force. The student council president's proposal essentially endorsed such a course of action.

"My thanks, but that won't be necessary. I prefer to fight my battles with only the pieces I hold in my hands."

What Sakayanagi wanted to know was how far she could go before it wasn't safe anymore. Just knowing that she could counterattack after being targeted was enough for her to go on.

"Satisfied?" asked Nagumo.

"Quite." Sakayanagi slowly stood, grasping her cane. "Ah, that reminds me—"

"You still have something you want to talk about?" asked Nagumo, adding that he couldn't give her much more time. Ignoring him, Sakayanagi kept going.

"This is merely me rambling now, but I happened to hear something quite interesting. Something about a student who was thinking of purchasing private points from third-years who are about to graduate, I believe. Purchasing the points that the school was going to collect and convert into currency after graduation. A powerful strategy, don't you think? A *winning* strategy."

The idea had come up during a conversation between Kouenji and Nagumo a few days ago, at the school camp. Although only boys had been around to hear it, Sakayanagi certainly could've heard it from one of the guys. In fact, it was almost inevitable they would want to share that information with her.

"Well, I made sure that strategy can't be used any-more...not that it's some novel concept that only Kouenji came up with or anything. More than a few students have thought about buying off surplus points from third-year students nearing graduation." Nagumo sneered. "It's been done many times before, yes. Which is exactly why the school announces the limited-time rule for 'purchasing their remaining private points upon graduation' from students in their third year. It's customary."

"Is that so? According to what I and others are told of the rules, private points are forfeited upon graduation. They become worthless. If that's the case, no wonder some third-year students consider entrusting their private points to an underclassman they're close to."

Many drops made an ocean. Even just inheriting private points from a few individuals would allow certain students to collect quite a hefty sum. It was no wonder that Nagumo had caught on to what Kouenji was doing, even at such an early stage.

"Normally," she continued, "this information is only disclosed to third-year students. Ignoring the matter of how you, President, came to know about it in your second year... I know why you discussed it so brazenly in front of all those first-years. You intend to have this limited-time rule changed, no?"

"I only did that because Kouenji seemed capable of paying more than the school itself offers. He was trying to monopolize points. That's foul play."

Openly announcing it in front of a group of boys from all grade levels made the school aware of the problem. A loophole in the rules. It was highly likely that additional rules would be put in place to discourage students from transferring private points.

Normally, no matter how wealthy a family someone came from, there was no guarantee they could cough up that much cash for points at graduation. Kouenji, however, was a rare exception.

It was clearly stated on the official website of the Kouenji conglomerate that Kouenji Rokusuke had accumulated an obscene amount of personal assets by his first year in high school. Even if he could go back on his deals, many would think it well worth the gamble with that much money on the line.

"However," said Sakayanagi, "the wealth he was born into could be considered one of the abilities at his disposal. Is he not allowed to put it to use?"

"By that logic, wouldn't anticipating his actions and forestalling them also be an exercise of abilities?"

Sakayanagi chuckled, lightly tapping her cane with every laugh. "I suppose so."

"From the beginning, I've never liked the school's rule about being able to move up to Class A with twenty million points. I'd like to have them revise it, if possible.

But then again...even if the system were to disappear in the future, I suppose it wouldn't apply to you first-years."

The school had clearly already informed Sakayanagi and the other first-year students of the rule's existence. They couldn't just withdraw the rule now that students were putting so much strategic thought into accumulating 20 million points.

"But there's never been a student who managed to accumulate 20 million points all by themselves, has there? If the rule is nothing more than a formality, then there's no need to worry about it, is there?" asked Sakayanagi.

"It just means that you can't save up the points by *yourself*."

"Yes, but saving up as a class also seems rather meaningless. Some students feared another class might send their spies to infiltrate their own, but that's not realistic. Even if a student from a lower class were somehow sent up to infiltrate Class A, they would naturally just betray their original, lower class after joining the superior one."

"True, there's no real benefit in deliberately trying to drag down a strong class. But who knows? There could be students out there with a strong sense of justice who'd stay loyal to their allies."

"But even so," said Sakayanagi, "it's not like the upper-ranked classes would simply hand information over to a new student who suddenly joined them. And the way this school is set up, any trouble you cause tends to come back to haunt you. If you intentionally sabotage your own class, you'll be expelled yourself. Am I right?"

Sakayanagi knew her stuff. Nagumo granted her a satisfied nod.

"I'll give you one friendly bit of advice. I don't ex-actly *dislike* your aggressive attitude, but if you start making enemies on all sides now, you're going to have a tough time later. Don't you think it'd be wiser for you to earn the trust of the people around you? It's not too late."

"And then use that trust as a weapon to achieve victory?"

"It's a far more efficient strategy." After all, nothing cut so deep as a knife in the back from a trusted friend. That was a fatal blow right there.

"Hmm. If you're telling *me* to build trust, then perhaps you've been too quick to toss aside the trust that you've so carefully built up yourself. As you just said, wouldn't it be far more effective to save that to use at the last minute?" asked Sakayanagi.

That declaration of war against the former student council president, made at the school camp ...that had been a betrayal of trust.

"I threw away that trust?" asked Nagumo, looking as

though he was holding back laughter. "I certainly lost the trust of Horikita-senpai and the students of third-year Class A. But nothing has changed with the second- or third-years from the other classes. The first-years will come to understand that soon too."

All of this was bluffing and hubris from Nagumo, Sakayanagi thought for a moment, but...perhaps not. Even breaking the rules that were established under Horikita Manabu had been part of his plan from the beginning. The second-years might've come to a consensus on the matter beforehand.

"And I *would* like to set the record straight, Sakayanagi. I recognize your ability. If you wish to join the student council at any time, I will allow it."

"Thank you very much. I'm glad I came here today. I think I understand you now, President Nagumo. At the very least, I'm relieved to see that we seem to be more compatible than I was with the former student council president." She bowed her head politely and stepped out of the student council office.

Nagumo followed. "You forgot your hat."

"Oh, my. Thank you very much." Sakayanagi bowed her head once again. "Now, if you'll please excuse me—"

"Sakayanagi, what do you know about Ayanokouji?" asked Nagumo suddenly.

"Ayanokouji...? I believe I've heard that name before. A first-year student, correct?"

"Yeah, I—it's nothing. Never mind," said Nagumo. If Sakayanagi didn't know, there was no point in talking.

Sakayanagi took a bold step forward. "I can do some investigating, if necessary. Hm?"

"Nah, I said too much. Forget it."

"I see."

On her way off from the student council office, Sakayanagi ran into a lone female student. Someone whom even a loner like Sakayanagi knew quite well. It was Kushida Kikyou, from first-year Class C. "Hello, Sakayanagi-san."

"My, what a coincidence. Do you happen to have some business in the student council office?"

"Mm. I was thinking about applying to join them. Were you thinking of doing the same thing, Sakayanagi-san?"

"Something like that. Now, if you'll please excuse me..."

"See you later."

Sakayanagi found it strange that Kushida would want to join the student council now, of all times. It *would* normally make sense for an honor student like her to join the council, but the timing made her suspicious. What Nagumo had done during the special exam was widely known, even among the girls.

The senior students knew the student council president well, and it wasn't surprising in the least that first-year students would have their suspicions about Nagumo's actions. If she knew about Ayanokouji Kiyotaka's true, hidden nature—if she were cooperating with him—it was possible she'd been sent here to investigate Nagumo.

But then again, considering Ayanokouji's personality, he probably wouldn't get so carelessly involved with Nagumo. Not at this stage.

Kushida Kikyou. She of the spotless reputation, that paragon of virtue.

"E he he he he. It's people like that, though, who always shock everyone by turning out to be the villains," muttered Sakayanagi.

At the very least, she didn't believe that Kushida was purely benevolent.

3

CHANGING RELATIONSHIPS

AN UNUSUAL SPECTACLE presented itself early one morning in Class C. A circle of girls seemed to have formed around Karuizawa Kei, all making so much noise that it bordered on total pandemonium.

"You're awfully late today, Ayanokouji kun," said Horikita Suzune, my neighbor. We had only about five minutes left until the morning bell rang to signal the start of class.

"I overslept."

"*Hm*," replied Horikita, disinterested.

Compared to our totally emotionless conversation, Kei's group was practically on fire.

"It sounds like Karuizawa-san broke up with Hirata-kun," said Horikita.

"Is that why they're all riled up today? A well-known couple broke it off?"

"They were polite enough to talk so loud the whole class could hear. So the information's been drilled into my head, whether or not I wanted it." She let out a heavy sigh, sounding annoyed. "You seem to be close with Hirata-kun and Karuizawa-san. Didn't you know?"

"It's not like I knew anything. It's their private business."

It hadn't seemed like she'd broached the topic yet back at the school camp, but I guess she'd gone ahead and done it after all. They'd been a well-known couple all through the whole school, so the news had really made some waves. Any third party hearing about it had to have been shocked.

Still, all this really meant was that Kei's and Hirata's connection had ostensibly severed. It didn't necessarily mean Kei had lost her position as the queen bee of the girls—though that might happen if someone else won Hirata's heart and became his one true love. Even then, I couldn't see Kei being pushed out of her position. If the other girls tried to disrespect her, Hirata himself would be the first person to put a stop to it. If not, there would have been no point in him going so far to save Kei as entering into a fake relationship with her.

"So who dumped who?" I asked Horikita. I didn't know the answer to that myself, so there was nothing for Horikita to be suspicious about.

"Seems like Karuizawa-san was the one who did the dumping."

"That's unexpected. She always seemed like the sort who'd want to date a good guy, like as a status thing."

"I suppose. That's what I thought, at the very least..." Horikita eyed me for a moment like she was suspicious of me, but looked away a moment later. She couldn't read my poker face, and the fact that she'd looked away was proof she was beginning to understand that, too.

Still...Kei broke up with Hirata, huh? Made sense, considering she'd started the whole fake relationship in the first place, and it didn't *really* matter who dumped who. It was probably Hirata who'd suggested that this arrangement would be better for Kei. If he'd been the one to dump Kei, it might've posed a danger to her status, suggesting there was something wrong with her.

Regardless, just looking around me made it obvious what a huge shock their breakup had been for Class C. What I really found incredible, though, was how openly the girls were discussing romantic affairs.

"Huh, what? You broke up with him, and you don't even have a new boyfriend lined up, Karuizawa-san?!" asked Shinohara, her words carrying loud and clear across the room.

Even though Ike, Sudou, and the other guys were chatting amongst themselves, they were clearly listening in on the girls' conversation.

"I don't know. I just think I need to step things up and move on. It would be easy to just let Yousuke-kun pamper me, but I've got a lot I want to think about on my own, you know?"

The catastrophic breakup of *the* couple obviously had an impact on Class C, but it might've had an impact on the other classes, too. If nothing else, the girls would certainly be fighting over who got Hirata next.

"I wonder how they can even think about things like romance. Considering the rules of this school, you'd think there'd be no guarantee what tomorrow brings."

"Maybe it's exactly because there's no guarantees that they're enjoying the present as much as they can."

"I have no reason to deny that, as long as they're not robbing someone else of their future..."

Hirata Yousuke, the other subject of this conversation, sat surrounded by guys and girls from our class, wearing his usual gentle expression. Even though he'd supposedly just been dumped by his girlfriend, he didn't look miserable at all. The clearest proof of that was that Ike and Sudou weren't heading on over to tease him.

No... It might be more accurate to say they'd graduated

from that sort of behavior. They did look interested in the conversation, but didn't seem to be whispering gossip. Actually, if anything, it was Horikita and I who were having a tasteless conversation.

After all the special exams and the training camp, those immature guys were starting to change, little by little. Of course, it wasn't as though everyone was maturing at the same rate.

"Yo, Hirata! I heard you got dumped by Karuizawa? Don't stress over it, dude! It's all good!"

I'd thought they were all capable of reading the room, but apparently, Yamauchi was the exception. He approached Hirata, all smiles, smacking him on the shoulder. The sight clearly made Ike and Sudou a bit uncomfortable, because they approached, flanking Yamauchi and grabbing him from the sides.

"Hey, what's the big deal? Come on, dudes, let's all console Hirata together!" said Yamauchi. "Even pretty boys can get dumped!"

"That's not cool, man," said Sudou. "Knock it off."

"Huh? But we're talking about the big heartthrob getting dumped. Extra spicy, extra rare!" Yamauchi just argued back, ignoring Sudou's attempt to chastise him.

"Sorry, Hirata. I'll get him outta here," said Sudou.

"It's okay," said Hirata. "It's the truth, isn't it?"

He would have been well within his rights to look displeased, but he didn't seem to mind at all.

From her seat beside me, Horikita spoke up suddenly. "That reminds me...what do you know about Ichinose-san? I've been hearing some things about her that sound like slander lately."

A question about Class B, out of the blue? Hmm.

"Maybe someone's spreading rumors because they're jealous of her? She's popular. Or maybe it's part of a strategy to bring down Class B. What do these slanderous rumors say?" I asked.

"I'm..." Horikita glanced around. "a little hesitant to say them out loud."

She passed me her notebook under the desk. Scrawled on the page was a whole list of things. Things like "She has a history of violent outbursts," "She's engaged in paid dating," "She's committed theft and robbery," and "She has a history of drug usage." Even the delinquents over there hadn't checked off all the items on this list.

"Those are some terrible rumors," I said.

"She doesn't seem like that kind of person at all, though..."

"Well, even if someone is starting rumors, I suppose they can't be charged with a crime."

"That's not true. Regardless of whether or not the defamatory statements are true or false, if they're spread publicly, and to enough people... it's defamation of character. You could sue," said Horikita.

"Sure, out in the real world." But this was high school. This was a self-contained space filled with students who were minors. It wasn't like these rumors were posted on the internet for the whole world to see.

"You're saying that it doesn't count as a crime at all, then?"

Well, even if it couldn't be punished through legal action, the school might still choose to issue some form of punishment at its own discretion. But it would probably be difficult to pinpoint precisely who had started the rumors. You could simply claim that you'd heard it from someone else, and that would be the end of it. The school's attempts to investigate would only go so far, and in the end, the problem would remain unresolved. All the school could really do was warn students not to thoughtlessly spread more rumors.

At any rate, it was clear that someone had been working to crush Ichinose for a while now. It was most likely Sakayanagi pulling the strings here, but barely anyone seemed to realize that.

"What has Ichinose been doing in response?" I asked.

"No idea. It's not like we're close. And if I carelessly step forward, suspicion might fall on us."

"Well, it's true that watching closely from the sidelines is the wisest option," I told her.

"Still...I have to wonder if a strategy this cliched will really work against Ichinose-san," mused Horikita.

"What do you mean?"

"No matter how bad the rumors are, the damage they can do is limited. Even I know what kind of reputation Ichinose-san has in this school. This kind of harassment is too vicious to be about something as everyday as envy, like you suggested."

"You're saying the culprit messed up?"

"I suppose. But, as the saying goes, 'where there's smoke, there's fire,'" she replied.

"So, you're saying that Ichinose has a history of violence, or did drugs, or something?" I asked.

"Even if the rumors are mostly baseless, maybe there's one in the mix that's true?" said Horikita, before adding, "Well, it's extremely unlikely, of course, but..."

Hmm. I guess there was no way to know yet whether everything was lies or nothing more than rumors, just as Horikita said. And Sakayanagi had hinted that there might be some truth to the rumors, even if just a shred of it.

"Well... it's not like we'll come up with answers just sitting here thinking about it. Enough about that. It seems the school has released updated class rankings based on the results of the school camp . Care to take a look?" asked Horikita.

"Meh, I don't really—"

"Yes, I'm aware you don't really care. But you really should know, just in case."

"Fine, fine."

I flipped through the pages of the notebook she'd forced me to look at.

3.1

THE UPROAR SURROUNDING Hirata and Kei's breakup that morning was still fresh in everyone's minds when Class C was rocked by yet more romantic drama. Classes had come to an end for the day, and some students were heading off to their clubs, while others went back to their dorms. In the midst of all that came an extremely unexpected visitor.

"Please excuse me," said the visitor. "Would Yamauchi Haruki-kun happen to be here?"

The students still in the classroom turned toward Yamauchi in unison, shock plain on their faces. As for Yamauchi, he'd probably been planning to head back to the dorm with Ike and play a game, because he'd just cracked open a strategy guide.

"Huh. Yeah, that's me," said Yamauchi, "but...what do

you want?" He usually got excited when he saw a cute girl, but this time? He seemed completely thrown.

The visitor was Sakayanagi, leader of the first-year Class A. And here she was, asking for Yamauchi by name. "Would you mind giving me a moment of your time?"

"O-of course! Uh, I don't mind. I'm free."

"Hm. But you know, I'm afraid that this isn't quite the place for this conversation. Why don't you meet me in the hallway by the stairs?"

Perhaps she was concerned about the looks she was getting from other students. Sakayanagi disappeared into the hall, her eyes cast downward. Silence fell upon Class C once more.

"No, no, no, *no*! This can't be happening!"

It was Ike—standing next to Yamauchi—who broke the silence. If Sudou were here, there probably would've been an even greater uproar, but he'd already left for basketball practice. Everyone in the room, including Yamauchi himself, struggled to wrap their heads around Sakayanagi's bold entrance and invitation.

Suddenly, as if moving purely on instinct, Yamauchi snatched up his bag. "Sorry! Got a little something to take care of!"

"Y-yeah, sure..."

But just as he was about to bolt from the classroom, Horikita blocked the exit, as if telling him to stop and think. "Wait, Yamauchi-kun—"

"Wh-what is it, Horikita?"

"Maybe she's trying to bring Class C down."

"Huh? Why do ya think that?"

"I could say that the fact that *you're* the one being invited out is abnormal, in and of itself." Horikita's face was serious, and her words were as pointed as knives. This was taking bluntness a bit too far. You couldn't blame someone for thinking she was insulting them.

But, on the contrary, Yamauchi was rather positive about the whole thing.

"You know that whole thing where you, like...fall in love with the transfer student after crashing into her at the street corner, and she falls over all cute, and she's holding toast corners in her mouth? Yeah. You know, right?"

"Toast...corners?" repeated Horikita. She furrowed her brow, confused. Who *wouldn't* be confused, with just Yamauchi's words to go on? But I'd seen him crash into Sakayanagi back at the school camp, so I figured that was the incident he was referring to.

"I'm going. Because Sakayanagi-chan is waiting for me."

Nothing Horikita could say was going to stop him. Yamauchi began walking off.

"What do you plan to do if this does happen to be a trap?" she asked.

"Nah, no way." He wasn't even considering the possibility. "I'm definitely our class's ultimate weapon, but that's why it's all going to be fine. If it's a trap—and that's a one-in-a-million chance—I'll just handle it, okay?"

He'd "handle it," huh? Handle it how? I bet he didn't even have a plan.

"...I understand," said Horikita. "I can't stop you. But please, don't get careless and leak any valuable information related to our class's internal affairs."

"Don't worry 'bout it. I know." And with that, Yamauchi left the classroom with a huge grin on his face. Some of the students, Ike included amongst them, hurriedly followed.

"We should go too," said Haruka, glancing not just at me, but at Keisei and Airi, who'd been sitting with her. I couldn't think of a reason *not* to go, so I nodded and got up from my seat.

Out in the hallway, we immediately ran into Ike and a few of the boys.

"Ah, stop, stop! Over here!" The Professor called out to us before we could move on. "Those two are talking over there, right now."

"Huh? What's up with the way he's talking?" Haruka muttered, noticing the Professor no longer spoke in the bizarre, archaic way that he used to.

"Seems like he got straightened out at the school camp," I answered, offering an explanation for the Professor's newly serious manner of speaking.

"It just feels like...I don't know, he's just less interesting. Ehh, who cares," said Haruka, almost immediately losing interest. We all focused our attention on Yamauchi and Sakayanagi.

"Umm, so. Uh. What did you wanna...talk about?" asked Yamauchi nervously.

As for Sakayanagi, she was running her left hand through her hair, looking somewhat embarrassed. If I had to analyze this situation from a psychological perspective, I'd say the hair thing was probably unconscious, meant to make her more attractive to the member of the opposite sex whom she was interested in.

"Wait," muttered Ike, sounding frustrated, "maybe Sakayanagi seriously does have a thing for Haruki?" He'd probably instinctively sensed that from Sakayanagi's expressions and gestures.

In this particular instance, however, I should probably assume that Sakayanagi was deliberately trying to give off that impression.

In contrast to my calm, collected analysis—

"No, no, this is way too stupid," Haruka spat. She looked sick to her stomach. "She's playing him. No way in hell that she could like Yamauchi-kun." A woman's intuition, maybe?

"Y-yeah, I think you're right," said Airi, perhaps because she could sense the same thing.

"Come on! Men are *so* simple. How could someone be fooled by that obvious act?"

"Is she...*really* acting?" asked Keisei uncertainly. I guess I wouldn't have noticed either if I hadn't looked carefully...

"*Definitely* an act," said Haruka, with absolute certainty.

"Maybe she's trying to get information about Class C, just like Horikita-san said?" said Ike.

"I don't know, seems a bit obvious," said Keisei. "You'd think there's a better way to do that. If she'd met up with Yamauchi in secret, it wouldn't put us on our guard like we are now. It would've made things way easier for her."

"Yeah, I suppose that's true..."

Keisei was exactly right. Even if she were planning to lure Yamauchi into a trap, there were plenty of ways to make contact with him without raising our suspicions. Deliberately making the entirety of Class C aware of her actions would do her more harm than good, implicating her in any problems that arose as a result.

So maybe she actually did have a thing for Yamauchi, just like Keisei and Ike had said. That would make more sense. But then again, Sakayanagi was aggressive and bold in general, so it really could be either one.

"To tell you the truth," said Sakayanagi, "I've been wanting to talk to you for a while now."

"F-f-f-for real?" sputtered Yamauchi. "Like, for real for real?"

"Well, I don't exactly have the kind of free time to lie about something like this, do I?" she replied.

I watched them carefully as they talked, conducting my own analysis.

"I'm afraid I can't quite calm myself down here, Yamauchi. Maybe we should...go somewhere else?"

"I-I see! Yeah, okay. Sure, let's!"

"Well, then, come along now, please."

The two of them walked side by side, Yamauchi trying to match Sakayanagi's slow pace. It seemed like he *was* capable of showing the bare minimum of consideration. The other students watched the pair walk away—they probably knew that trying to follow any longer would be difficult.

3.2

●●

ALL OF THE MEMBERS of the Ayanokouji Group had assembled in the café except for Akito, who'd headed to his club activities.

Haruka kicked things off at once. "Okay, so what do you think is *really* going on with that whole farce earlier? What're Yamauchi-kun and Sakayanagi-san *doing*?"

"Can we really say that it was a farce for certain though?" asked Keisei.

"That's...of course it was! Anyone would know. Right, Airi?"

"Well, um." Airi blushed. "I suppose. I think maybe it *could*..."

"Huh? But come on, it was so *obviously* put on, right? As a show? Right?" said Haruka.

"Yeah, I suppose that the gestures she made did make

it look one way... but like as Keisei-kun said, do you really think she'd come right out and do something bad by coming to visit Class C?"

"Come on," said Haruka, "use your head. That's part of the play; she wants to get us all mixed up with reverse psychology."

Hmm. So Haruka thought that by being so overt, Sakayanagi would make us think that it was way too obvious to be a trap in the first place. It was possible.

"What do you think, Kiyopon? Yukimuu? Do you seriously think there could be...romance?" asked Haruka.

"This is a topic that I'm not very well versed in," said Keisei. "I'll pass on further questions, thank you." He clearly didn't want to talk about romance any further.

Of course, now Haruka and Airi turned their gazes toward me.

"To be honest," I said, "Yamauchi and Sakayanagi haven't really interacted at all until now. This is way too sudden for something so basic to turn into romance, don't you think?"

"Quite the level-headed opinion, Kiyopon," said Haruka. "But falling in love doesn't always follow the same pattern or pace. People like Hirata-kun are one thing, I guess, but I doubt Yamauchi-kun is the kind who needs a while to fall for someone."

In the end, the conversation stalled out due to our lack of further information. Eventually, the topic changed from Yamauchi and Sakayanagi's romance to what was going on within Class C.

"Oh, speaking of Hirata-kun," said Airi, "didn't he break up with Karuizawa-san?"

"I can't really say I'm surprised," said Haruka. "Honestly, it seemed like they'd break up for sure someday."

"R-really, Haruka?" sputtered Airi.

"I guess if you look at it as the leader of the boys going out with the leader of the girls, then they make sense as a couple. But they're not really a good match for one another, y'know? It's just like, how do I put it...? Hirata-kun seems like he'd like a cute, gentle girl."

"But I think that Karuizawa-san is really cute," said Airi. "Don't you think so, Kiyotaka-kun?"

She was asking me? It was a difficult question. Perhaps she asked me that because she specifically wanted to hear *my* thoughts on that matter.

"Dunno," I said. "I've never really paid much attention to Karuizawa."

I didn't know how Airi felt about that, but it was the only answer I could give.

"Hmm, well, I *suppose* that's true." said Haruka. "Anyhow, Karuizawa-san aside, the problem is that Hirata-kun has become a free agent." Thankfully, she was shifting the topic of conversation back to Hirata. "It seems like there are quite a few girls in class who like Hirata-kun. I wonder what'll happen."

"Really?" asked Airi.

"Huh? You mean you never noticed? I mean...for example, Mii-chan definitely has a thing for him."

"Well... now that you mention it, she certainly does look over at Hirata-kun now and again."

"I know, right?"

Keisei took out his notebook, perhaps because he was getting fed up with all this talk of romance. "I'd like to study for a bit, I think."

"Oh, that's right, the year-end exam's coming up soon... Well, that's a depressing thought," said Haruka.

"I'll need to put together some study guides for you guys too," said Keisei.

Haruka let out a little laugh before lowering her head down on the table, like she was trying to make a full bowing motion. Chabashira hadn't given us any special instructions about the year-end exam, so it was probably going to be your standard written test. If a student got a failing grade, they'll be expelled at once. That was my guess, anyway.

"So when are we going to start our study group?"

"Let's see," said Keisei. "Hmm...how about after we've finished with the practice test on the 15th? That'll leave us about ten days until the final. If we focus on questions that have cropped up in the past and the trends we've been seeing in class, we should be good."

"Oh, ho!" Just like that, Haruka's mood seemed to lift, probably because this meant she could put off studying a little longer. "Just what I'd expect from you, Yukimuu! A perfect plan. Completely agree, let's roll with it."

"The last special exam of the school year will probably be held after the year-end final. In March, I expect," said Keisei.

"The last special exam of the year..." Airi echoed. "Wow, so our first year is already almost over, huh?"

"We've certainly been through a lot," said Haruka, "but it's really gone by so fast, hasn't it?"

Airi and Haruka both reflected back on the year for a moment...but Keisei brought them out of their reverie at once.

"It's way too early to be reminiscing. If you fail the year-end final exam, you'll get expelled. Not to mention what's in the special exam, too..." He probably didn't want them to lose focus.

Soon enough, Keisei was nose-deep in studying...and Haruka noticed something.

"Oh!"

I followed her line of sight, spotting Ichinose with what looked like several guys and girls, all Class B students. Unlike our own gathering, they all looked stiff and tense.

If I had to guess, they were trying to come up with ways to protect Ichinose from the defamation and slander currently directed her way. Ichinose herself, however, probably didn't want anything of the sort. She was behaving exactly the same as she always did: chatting with her friends, engaging cheerfully with people everywhere she went.

What concerned me was that Kanzaki wasn't around. He was Ichinose's close confidant, so I got the idea that they were together pretty frequently...

"It looks like she's in quite a bit of trouble right now," said Haruka, watching Ichinose with mild indifference, "doesn't it?"

"Some strange rumors are going around, I hear," said Airi. "I don't know who is spreading them, but they really are awful..."

"It's not really all that unusual though, is it?" asked Haruka. "I mean, yeah, this time things have gone a little too far, but I've seen similar stuff pretty often. You could say popular girls are just doomed to that fate, right?"

"You think so?" said Airi, a puzzled look on her face. "I didn't know that at all..."

"Sure. If you were more assertive and positive like Ichinose-san, you'd probably have a ton of people getting jealous of you. Don't you think, Airi?"

It was certainly possible. That being said, it didn't seem like Airi was even capable of picturing herself as the assertive type, no matter how hard she tried to envision it.

"Ehh, probably best not to worry about it," Haruka continued. "I bet Ichinose understands that too."

I just listened to them talk, not really participating in the conversation myself.

3.3

• •

ABOUT TWO HOURS LATER, the girls were chatting amongst themselves while Keisei pored over his notebook. I dipped in and out of the girls' conversation while I fiddled with my phone. And then, Haruka's phone vibrated where it sat on the table.

"Oh, it's from Miyacchi."

Haruka fiddled with the touchscreen options and answered the call on speaker phone.

"You finished with club stuff?" she asked.

"Sorry, think I'll be a little late." It was Miyake Akito, and he sounded nervous.

"Huh? Is practice running late or something?"

"No...no, I think some trouble's about to go down."

"Wait, trouble? What kind of trouble? Explain it to me so I can understand what's going on."

"Class A and Class B are going at it. If the worst-case scenario happens and a fight breaks out, I'll probably need to step in and stop it."

Sounded like Akito hadn't really gotten involved yet, but...Class A and Class B? The faces of the core members of Class B flashed through my mind. Would Ichinose really be so careless as to let a fight break out?

"Probably better to just leave it be," said Haruka. "It doesn't have anything to do with *our* class."

"Could be our problem tomorrow though," said Akito, before ending the call. Although normally a man of few words, he had a surprisingly passionate side to him. Like when he'd welcomed Ryuuen into our group at the school camp, despite no one else wanting anything to do with him.

"I wonder who's fighting...?" said Airi, sounding concerned.

"It's usually *that* class always starting fights. But not this time, I guess," said Haruka. She was referring, of course, to Ryuuen's class, now demoted to D.

"Me neither, now that I think about it," said Airi.

The two girls titled their heads to the side in apparent contemplation, thinking about this unexpected confrontation between Class A and Class B.

"Hey, Airi, Kiyopon, how about we head out and look for Miyacchi?" asked Haruka.

"B-But won't that be dangerous?" asked Airi.

"Well, sure, if things start to go down, our class might wind up getting dragged in as collateral damage," said Haruka with a teasing grin.

Airi shrunk back, looking a little frightened.

"But don't worry!" Haruka added. "Look, if something happens, I'm sure Miyacchi will do something, right? He used to be a pretty bad dude in the past, they say."

"B-bad? Really?"

"Well...by 'they say,' I pretty much just mean he says."

Hmm. Maybe that was why he didn't fear dealing with someone like Ryuuen—because he was confident in his own skills.

"Anyway, Airi," said Haruka, "if you get in trouble, I'm sure that Kiyopon will come save you. Right?"

"...I'll do the best I can," I said. "But I'd really rather not be in any fights."

"Aha ha ha! Well, no worries, right? It's not like things are going to ever get that violent here at this school. Uh. Probably..." Haruka trailed off vaguely, remembering the several instances of violence that had happened so far this school year.

Still, there wasn't really any reason to not look for Akito, so we decided to do just that.

3.4

W E DIDN'T SEE any sign of Akito as headed for the archery club.

"Huuuh? Where is Miyacchi, anyway?"

We were certain he'd been heading to the café, meaning he'd probably changed direction once he saw a fight brewing. We kept looking, and a few minutes later, we got some reliable information from a classmate who was heading back to the dorms from club activities.

And so we arrived at a spot by the side of the gym, a short distance from the school building, where we found two male students facing off against one another. Neither of them appeared to be the people whom Haruka and Airi had been expecting.

One of them was Hashimoto, from first-year Class A. The other was Kanzaki, from first-year Class B. Akito stood between them, as if trying to keep a handle on the situation.

"You guys aren't really going to fight, are you?" asked Akito.

"You're real persistent, Miyake. Besides, I wasn't the one trying to pick a fight here in the first place. Kanzaki dragged me into this," said Hashimoto. At that, my eyes met his. "Looks like your friends have arrived, huh?"

When he said that, Akito and Kanzaki looked over in our direction at almost the exact same time.

"...You guys came?" Akito didn't sound thrilled to have us sticking our noses in this. Well, I suppose there wasn't anything to be gained by getting the girls involved in this mess.

But Haruka spoke up, snapping back at Akito. "You're the one who stuck your nose into something weird, Miyacchi. We just came to save you."

"Save me..." Akito looked to the sky regretfully. "Of course."

"So, what's up? These two fighting?" asked Haruka.

Realizing there was no point arguing, Akito changed gears. "I was wrong about that. But it does seem like the situation is rather hostile."

"Kanzaki is the only hostile one," said Hashimoto.

It was certainly true that Hashimoto didn't seem to

be acting any differently than usual. But Akito wasn't taking Hashimoto's word for it. "I sure hope you're right about that."

Akito didn't seem like he was about to leave. Was a fight going to break out? He didn't seem sure either. Kanzaki, on the other hand, looked embarrassed to see us here, which suggested he didn't want anyone butting in.

Of course, he also knew he couldn't exactly just ask us to leave. In the end, he didn't say a word to us, but he turned back to Hashimoto once again.

"Picking up from where we left off before, Hashimoto," said Kanzaki. "What have you been doing after class? You're not in any clubs. Why are you hanging around so late?"

"Does not being in a club mean I gotta head back to the dorm right away? I'm free to do whatever I like after class. Besides, I think the only person present here who actually belongs to a club is Miyake. Right?" replied Hashimoto.

He assertively roped us into the situation, using us to poke a hole in Kanzaki's argument. Unlike Kanzaki, it seemed Hashimoto found our presence quite convenient.

We, the members of Ayanokouji Group, briefly exchanged looks.

We couldn't really say we were allies of Class A *or* Class B. Still, if we had to choose a side, it would inevitably be Class B because of the truce between Horikita and Ichinose.

Hashimoto grinned. "Ha! Can't give me an answer, Kanzaki, can you?"

"It's not as though you're here to meet with anyone," said Kanzaki. Though his expression remained as calm as ever, you could feel the force of personality behind his words. "You're just trying to grab random people and spread those rumors around, aren't you?"

So he'd been pressing Hashimoto about the Ichinose rumors, and it had made Akito worry they were going to come to blows. And now here we were.

Hashimoto seemed to sense that Kanzaki knew what he was up to, because he nodded. "Rumors? Oh, you mean the ones about Ichinose doing all kinds of bad stuff? What do those have to do with me?"

"Playing dumb is just a waste of time," said Kanzaki. "I'd like to make something clear to you, here and now: your actions are so underhanded that I see little difference between them and Ryuuen's."

"Okay, but even if you say that, I don't really know how I can answer you."

Hashimoto was being slippery and evasive in the face of Kanzaki's attempts to corner him. Akito, apparently having determined that they weren't immediately about to start throwing punches, came over to stand with us.

"Hey, what do we do now?" asked Haruka, directing her question to Akito in a low voice.

"Nothing. For the time being, we watch. If they go their separate ways without anything coming of it, that'll be that."

"But... Is it okay for us to listen to this?" asked Airi anxiously. I got where she was coming from; Class C had nothing to do with this discussion, and Kanzaki didn't seem happy that we were here.

"What do you think, Kiyotaka?" Akito asked me.

"Hmm. It's probably fine if we listen until they tell us to go, right? If it turns into a fight later, a third party like us could assert the legitimacy of the situation. Which should help Kanzaki, if he needs it," I reasoned.

Akito nodded in response, seemingly convinced.

But Hashimoto went on about the rumors, taking it a step further. "Hey, Kanzaki. These *rumors* about Ichinose...are you really sure they're just that? Just... rumors?"

"What?"

"You know how it goes: 'Where there's smoke, there's fire.' You can't blame somebody for looking for the fire, can you?"

"Rumors don't need a fire. Not if there's some sneak blowing smoke all over the place."

Hashimoto leaned back against a nearby wall. "I see. Well, it's certainly true that fires and rumors are separate things." Proverbs didn't always hold true in the real world. "But can you say with absolute certainty that Ichinose doesn't have a dark past, Kanzaki?"

"One year, Hashimoto. We've struggled together in Class B for about one year, through thick and thin. So... yes, I *am* certain."

"Oh, please! Enough already, Kanzaki. You're so corny, I can't even look you in the eye." At that, Hashimoto lowered his gaze mockingly.

"Of course, I've also asked Ichinose directly."

"Oh? And what did she say?"

"She told me not to worry, and not to be misled by all these rumors."

"In other words, that means she neither confirmed nor denied anything?"

"That's true. That's why I decided to believe her."

"Dude, come on. Seriously? How much of a bleeding heart can you possibly be?" sneered Hashimoto. He kept going. "No one *wants* to talk about their own dark past, and nobody's going to tell the whole truth just because a friend asks. Of course she wouldn't tell her classmates the truth. Or what, do you think that just because she's a good person now, she was a good person in the past?"

Kanzaki didn't appear to be shaken at all by his words. No, the look in his eyes was of complete trust in Ichinose.

Hashimoto didn't stop. "Just because you're Ichinose's right-hand man, you think she's gonna tell you everything? Come on, how naïve can you be?"

Undisguised disgust at Kanzaki's blind faith dripped from every word. That, or he'd decided that there was no point in dragging out this confrontation.

"I'm not talking about that," said Kanzaki. "I want you to tell me about yourself. About what you've been doing today."

"All right, fine. I'll tell you. Yeah, I've been spreading rumors about Ichinose," Hashimoto admitted. "Look, Kanzaki...you're smart. You're a caring guy. But that's why you shouldn't get so involved in this. You can only blindly believe others, you know? This just...isn't your place."

"You're saying you have no intention of retracting those rumors, then."

"Retract the rumors? C'mon, don't you think you're getting it twisted? There's no *retracting* rumors. They spread wherever they will. I just happened to encounter them along the way and help pass them on," said Hashimoto.

So he admitted to spreading the rumors but flatly denied being their source. Still, Kanzaki wasn't backing down.

No...he seemed to already know that Hashimoto wasn't the source.

"I've been conducting a thorough investigation of the students of Class A over the last few days."

"And?"

"I've traced the source of all of the rumors back to a number of guys and girls from first-year Class A. When I pressed those students about where they'd heard the rumors, they responded with vague answers like 'I don't remember' or 'I heard them from somewhere.' Much like the answer you just gave me right now. Every one of them. I'm sure that you, of all people, must understand what that means, Hashimoto."

Someone had given instructions to those students.

"Sorry, Kanzaki," said Hashimoto, "but I haven't got the faintest clue. If you don't mind, why don't you say it outright?"

"The rumors meant to defame Ichinose were almost certainly spread by first-year Class A."

"Huh."

"Don't try to weasel out of it. I didn't just ask the first-year students—I asked the second-years and third-years too. They said they heard the rumors from *your* class. Exactly where I'd traced them back to. If necessary, I can call those students and have them confirm the facts in person."

Apparently, Kanzaki and the rest of Class B had thoroughly investigated the source of the rumors. He was convinced first-year Class A had spearheaded their creation, which was why he was now confronting Hashimoto. The fact that he was working alone probably meant that he was trying to avoid causing trouble for Ichinose. If a large number of students caused a commotion, it would get the attention of students who hadn't initially been interested in the rumors.

Then again, it was entirely possible that Kanzaki was just handling this case entirely on his own.

"I see. So that's why you've been stalking me again today." Hashimoto shrugged and let out a sigh.

"Again," huh? So he'd noticed Kanzaki tailing him some time ago. Although it didn't seem like he really cared about being followed, probably because he didn't see it as a real threat.

"Was it Sakayanagi who told you to spread those rumors?" asked Kanzaki.

"Uh, no?"

"Okay, then who? The only other person who could give out orders to Class A would be Katsuragi."

"Who knows? I've just been hanging out with other students. I picked up the rumors somewhere along the way. Even if you say that the rumors came from Class A, what am I supposed to do with that? Maybe it's Ryuuen's handiwork. Maybe he's just been pretending to be in retirement?"

After hearing that, Kanzaki changed his approach. "So you took stories without knowing whether or not they were actually true, accepted them at face value, and just... spread them around?"

"That's just how people work, isn't it? It doesn't matter if they're true or made up; if the rumor is interesting, people are going to talk. Besides, us guys are nothing compared to the girls in that department, eh?" Hashimoto directed his gaze over at Haruka and Airi.

"Well... I certainly do like rumors, but..."

"And sadly, the juicier the rumors, the more exciting they become. Try to think this through a little more objectively, Kanzaki. Ichinose neither confirmed nor denied the rumors. And she's not asking anyone to help her, either. Don't you think that's strange? If they're a complete fabrication, then you'd think she'd be asking for help finding their source, right?" said Hashimoto.

"Ichinose has an extreme aversion to conflict," said Kanzaki. "I believe she could find it in her heart to show compassion to everyone...even those who spread vicious rumors about her."

Since she wasn't taking a stance of her own on the

subject, Kanzaki couldn't do anything but choose to believe in her.

"God, you Class-B people..."

In any case, Hashimoto's words and behavior had led me to one conclusion: the rumors being circulated about Ichinose...weren't all lies, after all.

I put aside my position as a student for a moment, examining this case from a social perspective. Ichinose could probably sue the person(s) who'd started the rumor for defamation of character. Regardless of whether the rumors were true, they'd damaged her reputation, which gave her grounds to sue.

...Unless, of course, the rumors involved facts that were already public knowledge. If this *was* Sakayanagi's handiwork, then it was all going according to plan. Ichinose's silence was proof it was working as intended.

After giving Kanzaki a pat on the shoulder, Hashimoto thrust his hands into his pocket and tried to walk off.

"We aren't done talking," said Kanzaki.

"Come on, man, isn't this enough? Even if we continue this conversation, it's not like we're going to see eye-to-eye," said Hashimoto.

He gave Haruka and Airi a gentle wave, then headed off in the direction of the school building. Something was off, here. My gut told me Hashimoto was acting differently around me than he had when we were at the school camp.

It was nothing more than a hunch, though. I couldn't put a finger on what, specifically, had changed.

"Please excuse me." Kanzaki offered us a slight bow, and then walked back toward the dorms rather than the school building.

"Wow, okay," said Haruka. "That right there? That was *awesome.*"

"What on earth," said Akito, "was *awesome* about that?"

Haruka stuck out her tongue. "Come on! It's like, you know, we were on the verge of things getting exciting. Besides, even in the off chance that we got attacked, you could've totally taken the dude, right, Miyacchi?" She made a few quick jabbing motions in the air to demonstrate.

"I hear you used to be a delinquent?" I asked, following the flow of the conversation.

Akito let out a heavy sigh. "Don't tell people that, Haruka. I don't really want it getting around."

"Come on, what's the big deal?" she asked. "You're different now, anyway. You were really strong then, huh?"

"I...I wasn't some famous delinquent or anything, okay? Someone else was top dog at the junior high I went to. That guy was way stronger than me."

"Huh. Was it a pretty rough school?"

"Well yeah. That's just how people were in my hometown. I mean, the adults, too. And when they had kids, they'd raise 'em to be the same. Oh, by the way, Ryuuen from Class D? He used to go to a junior high next to mine," said Akito.

"Whoa, seriously?!"

"Yep. We ran into each other a few times when fights broke out between the schools. I don't think the guy really paid me any mind, though."

Akito probably knew how to handle those kinds of situations because he'd had experience brawling.

"Okay," he said, "the conversation ends here. And don't spread this outside the group, okay?"

"Okay, okay, I get it," said Haruka. "How about we head back to the café? Yukimuu is waitin' for us."

"Gotcha."

At the end of the day, this was Akito's business, after all. If I was sure of anything, it was that it was best not to dig any deeper.

4 ► UNCHANGING INTENT

THAT THURSDAY, I spied Ichinose while heading back to the dorms. She was usually surrounded by a gaggle of students, both guys and girls, but she seemed to be alone right now, which was rare. For some reason, I didn't sense her usual bubbliness from her either.

I wondered if she was alone because she was keeping her distance from her friends right now, rather than by mere coincidence. She was currently the person with the most concentrated attention focused on them in our school, regardless of grade level, and anyone she carelessly got involved with might take collateral damage themselves. I wouldn't be surprised if she'd made the decision to stay away from her friends as a result.

I thought back to Kanzaki's and Hashimoto's conversation from the other day. Should I try calling out to her?

I considered doing so but then sensed someone behind me and decided to refrain. I took out my cell phone and turned on the camera, switching from the rear-facing lens to the front-facing one and using the image on my screen to casually examine what was behind me.

Two students on their way back to the first-years' dorm, just like me. One was Hashimoto. He seemed to be walking normally, but after what happened the other day, I couldn't assume it was a coincidence. Was he following me?

While I was trying to ascertain that, however, the other student approached me without hesitation. I closed the camera app and returned my phone to my pocket as she drew near.

"U-um, excuse me, Ayanokouji-kun. Do you have a minute...?"

It was my classmate, Wang Mei-Yu. People tended to call her Mii-chan because her name was difficult to pronounce, though I found it a little embarrassing to call her that, even in my head.

"Do you... have a little time right now? I was hoping I could talk to you about something," she said.

She wanted to talk to me? We'd barely had any contact at all so far. In fact, this was practically the very first time she'd ever spoken directly to me. It didn't seem like there was anyone else around whom she could be addressing, though...

Ichinose continued getting further away, without noticing me. At this point, running on over and chasing after her would just look strange.

"I'm sorry, you're probably busy, aren't you...?"

"No, I was just heading back to the dorms. It's okay."

Mii-chan brightened when I said that, releasing a sigh of relief. Hashimoto passed by us and continued in the direction of the dorms, not looking in my direction and not calling out to me.

"So... You said you wanted to talk to me?" I asked.

"Well, talking here will be a little awkward..." Mii-chan looked around the surrounding area, fidgeting. Apparently, this wasn't a topic for casual conversation.

"Okay." Of course, it wasn't like I could go, "Oh, since the dorms are so close, how about you come to my room?" And going to Mii-chan's room myself seemed even more far-fetched. "What do you want to do, then?"

I left the decision to Mii-chan, who thought it over, then suggested, "Would...the café be okay? We might be a little late heading back after, though."

If that was what she wanted, I had no reason to decline. She said we'd be a little late, but it was only a difference of about five or ten minutes on foot, which wasn't a big deal.

In accordance with Mii-chan's suggestion, therefore, we headed on over to the Keyaki Mall Café. That being said, we didn't know each other very well. We walked some distance apart from one another, rather than close together.

4.1

THE CAFÉ WAS ALWAYS PACKED, and today was no exception. Even I, who lacked common sense about the details of normal high school life, understood why. It was extremely popular, especially with girls, and owned by a major company in the outside world. Their drinks were pricey—too pricey for your average high school student to indulge in more than a few times a month, unless they worked a part-time job.

But students at this school received allowances based on their class points, meaning many could afford to patronize the café as often as they liked, as long as they weren't in dire straits or anything. As a result, the café was inevitably packed, day in and day out.

We still managed to find open seats, though, and sat down, facing one another. Mii-chan stared at the drink she'd ordered, making no attempt to look me in the eye.

She reminded me of Airi. If I inadvertently put pressure on her, it would probably make it even harder for her to speak her mind. I decided against attempting to break the ice. To give her room to marshal her thoughts, I said I was going to get some sugar.

I went over to the counter, where I took one sugar packet. Without letting my eyes wander around the room, I confirmed that Hashimoto had also found his way to the café.

I doubted he'd had a sudden craving for a caffeine fix. He was following me, without a doubt. Had Sakayanagi told him to keep an eye on me? No, that didn't seem right. Sakayanagi didn't want word about me to get around. And if she did want to tail me, she'd use her puppet, Kamuro. Assuming Sakayanagi understood what kind of person Hashimoto was, she'd know he wasn't the right choice for tasks like these. She'd want to avoid carelessly giving Hashimoto information about me, only for him to leak that information to a third party.

Was he following me of his own accord, then? I didn't recall doing anything during the school camp to warrant that. I should have come across as nothing more than just another member of the group.

Ryuuen, Ishizaki and Albert, and Ibuki. I wondered if they'd been talking to anyone, but then nixed that possibility. Well, I wasn't going to solve this mystery right now. It did seem like it was going to become a problem I'd have to deal with before long, though.

I decided to ignore it for now in favor of continuing my conversation with Mii-chan. It had been about a minute since I'd left my seat across from her, which I now retook. Almost immediately after, Mii-chan broke the silence.

"Um... Well, it's about Hirata-kun."

About Hirata-kun, huh?

"I was hoping you could tell me some things..." she continued.

"We're not really all that close," I replied almost immediately, as if taking precaution. But Mii-chan looked at me with surprise.

"Then why did Hirata-kun tell me you're the most reliable person in class, Ayanokouji-kun?"

"...Is that so?"

"Yeah. He said that you're the most dependable person in class. He really spoke highly of you."

While I was honestly happy to be praised by Hirata, if that kind of talk got around, it would spell trouble. That said, I could understand why Hirata had given Mii-chan my name. There were plenty of students you could count on, but if you restricted your search to Class C, well, things got a little complicated. If you further narrowed your criteria to only include guys, then it wasn't so odd that Hirata had named me.

Still...she wanted to talk about Hirata, huh? In light of the earlier conversation with Haruka, I could guess what this was about.

"So, um, Hirata-kun and Karuizawa-san, well... They broke up recently. Did you know that?"

"Yeah, of course." I pretended to have no idea why she was bringing that up.

"W-well, um..." Mii-chan faltered a few times, then finally got to the heart of the matter. "...D-do you know if there's anyone that Hirata-kun likes right now?"

Yep, there it was. What was the correct course of action in a scenario like this? I mulled it over for a moment, then decided it would be best to just give her an honest answer.

"I don't think so."

"R-really?"

"I can't say for absolutely certain, of course. But as far as I know, no, there isn't anyone. Besides, he only just got dumped by Karuizawa. It's probably too soon for him to have feelings for someone else," I replied.

"That's certainly true," replied Mii-chan, seeming to grow calmer.

"Is it okay if I ask you one thing, just out of curiosity?"

"S-sure."

"When did you start liking Hirata?"

"Huuuuuh?!"

Was that an odd question? Mii-chan's face had gone bright red. She looked completely flustered.

"Wh-wh-wh-why are you asking me that?"

"Well, if you don't want to answer, you don't have to—"

"...Right after the entrance ceremony, I think?" she replied, cutting me off.

So, she'd told me anyway, huh.

"I'm a little clumsy..." She'd fallen in love with Hirata the very first time she'd met him, Mii-chan went on to candidly explain. "...I guess. That's what it feels like, anyway."

"Is that so?" There was a lot I didn't understand, but I was sure of one thing: she'd been charmed by Hirata's gentleness.

"But—" Mii-chan had blushed as she spoke about meeting Hirata, but now her expression grew cloudy, like she'd snapped back to reality. "I... I don't think someone like me could be Hirata-kun's girlfriend..."

"Why?" I asked, wondering how she could be so sure of that.

"Because there are too many rivals out there... And besides, I've never been in love before or anything..." she replied.

So despite overflowing with feelings of love, she didn't have the courage to make a move? I didn't want to believe the absence of romantic experience was necessarily a handicap, but I couldn't say for certain that it had no effect at all.

"Well, Mii-chan... Wait, it's probably not okay for me to be calling you Mii-chan, is it?"

"Oh, no, it's completely fine. Everyone calls me that. Even though both my parents are Chinese, they seem to like my Japanese nickname, so they call me Mii-chan too."

In other words, she wasn't half-Japanese. "Are you studying abroad?" I asked.

"Um, well, when I was in my first year of junior high, my father came to Japan on business," she answered.

So she'd moved here with her family? "Did you encounter any obstacles? Like dealing with a language barrier, for example."

"It was really at first. I was more worried about whether I could make friends than learning the language... But lots of people spoke good English at the junior high I enrolled in, so we got along pretty well," she explained.

That reminded me—I'd heard Mii-chan was good at English. On top of that, she'd also perfectly mastered Japanese in her three years of junior high. I'd heard Chinese students had to keep their noses to the grindstone to make it in a society that was far more competitive than Japan's. It was probably precisely because she'd received such a rigorous education that Mii-chan had been able to smoothly integrate into Japan. All that remained was for her to improve her communication skills, like Airi.

"I wonder if someone like me even has a chance..."

"I don't want to make any irresponsible statements, but I think you should have a decent chance. Don't you?"

"Really?"

"I'm not lying about that. But..."

"B-but?"

Though this might make her more anxious, I should probably tell her about a rather difficult part of this equation. "Hirata's a good guy, right?"

"Yeah."

"Don't you think that's exactly why, the next time he goes out with someone, he'll be really careful? Right? He might even feel responsible for what happened, like he wasn't able to make Karuizawa happy or something."

"I see..." she replied, nodding. "You're right. And I don't think...I could confess my feelings to him right away either."

"You might be concerned about the competition out there, but if you get impatient and confess your feelings too soon, there's a high chance you'll be rejected," I told her.

I advised her to take things slow and steady. She was going to have to ask Hirata how he felt before she could be sure of anything, but I couldn't picture him pointlessly rushing into dating another girl right now. It was far more likely that he would reject the majority of the girls who happened to confess their romantic feelings to him right now. In that sense, Mii-chan had a better chance of winning if she waited.

"...I think I might have been mistaken about you, Ayanokouji-kun."

"Mistaken?"

"Well, it's just, you don't normally talk all that much. Or at all, really. You kind of give off this scary vibe. But after meeting with you face-to-face, and talking like this, I feel like you're super easy to talk to. It feels like you really care about my problems, I guess..."

Despite her compliments, the truth was that I wasn't *really* listening to her. It would be more accurate to say I was subconsciously analyzing our conversation, carefully scrutinizing it for information that might be helpful to me later, or something that I could use. If I came off like

I really cared about her problems, then that was a convenient bonus, no more.

Should I go a little bit further? It seemed this might be a good opportunity to ask her about a number of different things.

"Oh? Mii-chan and... Ayanokouji-kun, is that you?"

Just as I opened my mouth, Shiina Hiyori, from first-year Class D, appeared at our table. I closed my mouth without a word.

"Hello, Hiyori-chan," said Mii-chan. Judging by the way they referred to each other, they were close.

"Are the two of you here on a date, by any chance?" asked Hiyori.

"N-n-no, that's not it at all, Hiyori-chan!" said Mii-chan, panicked, quickly rising to her feet. She waved her arms before her to signal her rejection of the idea, a gesture so expansive that her entire body shook with the motion. The fact that she would deny it so excessively kind of stung.

"In that case, would it be all right if I joined you?"

"Of course, that's fine with me. ...Is it okay with you, Ayanokouji-kun?"

"Sure."

"Thank you very much." Hiyori sat down next to Mii-chan, wearing a wide and happy smile. "It's rather unusual to see the two of you together. What were you talking about?"

"U-Um, well..." Mii-chan struggled to admit that we were talking about her crush.

"I'm interested in China, so I was asking her about it," I replied.

"In...China?"

"Yeah. It's a country I'd like to visit sometime, and so I thought I'd talk to Mii-chan, a Chinese person."

I shot a look over at Mii-chan, basically saying "Right?" with my eyes. She nodded quickly several times in response.

"China is really nice, isn't it? I'm also really interested in it, especially things like the Great Wall." Hiyori put her hands together in front of her, still smiling. Surprisingly enough, it seemed this was a topic she was really into.

"I suppose you can't really avoid mentioning the Great Wall when you talk of China. But personally, I'd like to visit the Ancient City of Ping Yao," I replied.

"Ping Yao?"

It seemed Hiyori hadn't heard of that before. On the other hand, Mii-chan's eyes widened in surprise at hearing me mention it.

"Wow. It's a World Heritage Site, but still...I'm impressed that you know it..." she said.

"I just happened to hear about it is all."

"By the way, are you two...friends?" asked Mii-chan, seeing Hiyori and I speak so naturally to one another.

"Yes. We're reading buddies."

"Well, you're not wrong about that, I guess."

"Reading buddies...?" repeated Mii-chan. She looked puzzled for a moment, like she didn't get what we meant, but then immediately turned that confusion into positivity. "It's wonderful to have friends in other classes, isn't it?"

She probably hadn't had any friends outside her own class before the school camp.

"I think so too. I think there's more to life here at school than just antagonizing each other," said Hiyori.

Competing with other students was fundamental to how the Advanced Nurturing High School worked. Many students here had a strong tendency to see people other than their classmates as rivals. However, now that we'd gotten this far, more and more of them had started to open up to people outside their own class.

That said, the school was still keeping parts of its agenda hidden from us. If not, it wouldn't have implemented rules like the ones at the training camp. I couldn't say with any certainty that the inter-class mingling wouldn't have a negative impact down the line.

If the time came when you were forced into a competitive situation, a half-hearted acquaintanceship could do more harm than good.

"THANK YOU for everything today, Ayanokouji-kun," said Mii-chan.

"No, I should be the one thanking you, since I just dominated the conversation asking you about China and all." I reflexively expressed my thanks to her in response, causing Mii-chan to scratch her cheek with her finger, appearing embarrassed.

"Ah, w-well, I suppose," she replied.

"I'll head on up after taking a look at my mail," I said aloud, turning my back toward Mii-chan and Hiyori as they were about to get on the elevator.

I checked the contents of my mailbox once or twice a week, as I was sure many other students did. A lot of what arrived in our mailboxes was from the school, but people sometimes received packages via personal correspondence. There were also times when things students had mail-ordered were routed to them through the school.

But I wasn't checking my mailbox for anything so ordinary.

"Nothing today either, huh?"

I had started checking my mail regularly ever since my father came to visit the school, anticipating he might try to contact me. Since I saw nothing of note, I headed back to the elevator. When I got there, I saw Hiyori there waiting for me.

"Do you have a minute?" she asked.

"Yeah."

We headed over to stand by the sofa in the lobby, a short distance from the elevator.

"There was something I had wanted to ask you earlier, but since you were with Mii-chan..." said Hiyori, trailing off. She briefly scanned our surroundings to see if anyone was around, and then spoke again. "Have you heard anything about Ichinose-san?"

"Meaning what? If you're referring to those bizarre rumors, then yeah, I've heard about those."

"Exactly that. Do you happen to know who's spreading those rumors?" asked Hiyori.

"No... I'm afraid I don't."

It would have been easy to name Sakayanagi or Hashimoto, but I thought I'd avoid doing that.

"To be honest, I really hate seeing Ichinose-san being tormented like this. She treats even students like me, who don't have many friends, the same as she would anyone else," said Hiyori.

If I'd remembered correctly, Hiyori and Ichinose had been in the same group at the school camp. I supposed she might feel a stronger bond with Ichinose than with other students after eating the same meals and sleeping in the same room.

"Ayanokouji-kun." There was a kind of determination in Hiyori's eyes. "I dislike hurting others. However, I believe that it's sometimes necessary to fight in order to protect your friends."

"I suppose that's right. You can't possibly save everyone."

"Even though Ichinose-san is a mutual enemy of ours, there must be a way to help her. I don't have a plan yet, but... Will you help me?"

"Help, huh? In that case, you should talk to Horikita."

"Horikita-san?" Hiyori didn't seem thrilled by the prospect.

"I suppose Class C might also be willing to help Ichinose," I added. If that happened, it would mean Classes D, C, and B were joining forces against Class A.

But Hiyori wasn't jumping for joy at this prospect either.

"So you won't do anything yourself, Ayanokouji-kun?"

"I have no influence whatsoever over Class C."

"Is that so?" she replied, tilting her head to the side with a puzzled look on her face.

"For the girls, it's Horikita. For the guys, it's Hirata. You'll just have to talk to one of them about it," I answered.

"I see..." said Hiyori. Her shoulders slumped, seemingly in disappointment.

"Dissatisfied?" I asked.

"No...Well, it's just that I barely know Horikita-san or Hirata-kun, So I thought that if I went to you, Ayanokouji-kun, then..." She slumped her shoulders even further, looking despondent. I was surprised by the sight.

"Sorry. If there's nothing I can do, then there's nothing I can do."

"No, no, it's okay... It was a selfish idea on my part. I just came up to you and asked without considering how you might feel," she replied, bowing to me.

"Well, do you want me to put in a word in with them on your behalf, for the time being?" I asked.

"Really? You would do that for me?" Even though that was exactly what Hiyori had just said she wanted, she seemed to have changed her mind. "I'm sorry, but...

on second thought, let's just meet another time. If we act carelessly, it might make the rumors spread even further and cause more trouble for Ichinose-san."

"I see. Yeah, you might be right about that."

As of this moment, there was no telling what the people targeting Ichinose might do next. Moving incautiously might do more harm than good.

Not to mention the possibility that the rumors about Ichinose were closer to the truth than many might think...

4.3

AFTER RETURNING TO MY ROOM, I received a text from Horikita.

Do you have a minute now?

I didn't respond, but when she saw the read receipt on her text, she sent another right away.

Since the message I just sent was marked as read, I'm just going to go ahead and keep talking. Ichinose-san is coming to my room tonight. Are you coming too?

Now that was unexpected. I'd planned to just read her messages, but now decided to actually respond. *What led to this?* I texted back.

We have an alliance with Class B. It's only natural that we'd want to lend a hand when the situation calls for it. But in this case, we're not getting the full story. So I was thinking we'd hear it from the person in question, replied Horikita.

In other words, she'd contacted Ichinose and asked if they could meet in person, huh? A bold move.

It would be easy for me to refuse. Horikita would probably tell me what they talked about if I asked her later. That being said, Horikita might not get the whole story out of Ichinose. Even Kanzaki didn't know everything about her, despite how close they were.

If that was the case, would I get closer to the truth if I met with Ichinose directly and asked her myself? Unfortunately, I couldn't do so without getting involved in whatever happened next.

What should I do? After giving it some thought, I sent Horikita a short response.

What time?

Seven.

That was a little late. I'd have to be careful to not be seen by other students.

Got it. I'll let you know before I head over.

And so, I decided to meet Ichinose together with Horikita.

4.4

I SPENT THE REST of the time leisurely hanging out in my room. At five minutes to seven, I left my room and walked over to Horikita's. At almost the exact moment I got off the elevator, I spied Ichinose.

"Ah, good evening, Ayanokouji-kun," said Ichinose.

I responded to her with a light wave.

"Sorry for the bother," I told her.

"Aha ha! No no, I'm the one being a bother." With those words, Ichinose took the lead and rang the bell to Horikita's room. We heard the lock click open at once.

"Please come in."

We planned to meet at seven; there was nothing odd about us arriving at the same time. Horikita invited us in without comment, and I went ahead and sat down on the floor. I had visited her room before, and it didn't seem to have changed much since the last time. It was much like mine: simple and austere.

"I'm sorry to call you over like this on a weeknight, Ichinose-san."

"You're doing this out of consideration for me, though. There's no need to be sorry," Ichinose said.

Seeing her face-to-face like this, she seemed like the same old Ichinose she'd always been.

"But...if this goes on too late, it'll affect us tomorrow, so I don't plan to draw out this conversation. So I'm sure you've heard some worrisome rumors going around about me."

"Yes. Do you know who is spreading those rumors?" asked Horikita, getting straight to the point. I listened, curious to see if Ichinose would answer the question honestly.

"I don't have any hard evidence. But if I had to guess, I'd peg Sakayanagi."

A much more direct answer than I'd expected. I doubted Ichinose would have named a specific person if she was less than halfway certain; she wasn't the type to suspect others without good reason. This made something very clear to me: if nothing else, Ichinose was aware of the identity of the person who was spreading rumors about her.

"Sakayanagi-san... What makes you so sure that she's the one?" asked Horikita.

"To put it simply, it's because she declared war on us. Is that not enough to convince you?"

Horikita probably already knew how aggressive Sakayanagi could be. Considering the fact that she'd been willing to deepen the rift within her own class to bring down Katsuragi, one could easily imagine her taking aim at Class B's leader, Ichinose, in order to defeat them.

"No. That is enough." It was precisely because Horikita thought the same way that I did that she saw no need to pry further. "So, she's circulating baseless rumors about you to damage your character?"

"Hm... How do I put this?"

"Are you not going to deny the rumors?"

"I'm sorry, Horikita-san. I can't answer that question. You and Ayanokouji-kun are my friends, but you belong to a different class. Even if we say we're allies now, we're still destined to compete with each other someday, right?" said Ichinose.

Direct as Ichinose's first answer had been, it seemed she was declining to answer this question. Well, that was only to be expected.

"I don't intend to force an answer from you. But you

do know that silence can be interpreted as you saying the rumors are true, right?" said Horikita.

"Everyone is free to interpret the rumors that way, including you, Horikita-san. But I have absolutely no intention of overreacting to this situation. Sakayanagi's strategy is to get Class B all riled up. I think the best possible countermeasure is to stay silent," replied Ichinose, smiling, looking the same as she always did.

Harassment of this sort happened everywhere, all the time. There was no foolproof way of dealing with it: you could react or stay silent, but at the end of the day, the peanut gallery would cause as much of a ruckus as they wanted. But perhaps it was precisely because of the rampant speculation she knew people would engage in that Ichinose had chosen not to react, but rather to simply wait for things to pass.

"The reason I wanted to meet with you today, Horikita-san, was to talk to you about this whole thing. I don't want you to get dragged into it. Even if I stay silent, it'll take longer for the situation to blow over if people around me make a fuss. More importantly, though, there's no need for Class C to end up in Sakayanagi's crosshairs just because they tried to help me. I'll be just fine," said Ichinose, giving us a vigorous nod, her smile not fading at all.

"...I know that you have a strong heart. Regardless of their veracity, anyone would be affected by having such vile rumors about them do the rounds. But despite that, you aren't thinking about yourself. You're showing consideration for the people around you," said Horikita.

"I'm really not that great," said Ichinose, sounding a little bashful now. "You and your class should carry on as you have been, Horikita-san. I'll clean up my own mess."

Saying that, she quickly stood up. It seemed she'd only come here to caution Horikita not to get involved.

"Do you know about Kanzaki and the others?" I asked. My input was probably unnecessary, but I thought I'd try something.

"Kanzaki-kun?"

"He confronted Hashimoto from Class A the other day, asking him point-blank to stop spreading the rumors. Well, I guess it might have gone a bit beyond simply asking."

"I see... Kanzaki-kun is really kind. I told him he didn't need to do anything."

"It's not just Kanzaki-kun, though. I'm sure more of your classmates are trying to take action for your sake," said Horikita. Though this was the first time she'd heard mention of what Kanzaki did, I was willing to bet she was right on the money.

"I'll have a talk with my classmates again. Is it okay if we call it a night and end our conversation here?" asked Ichinose.

"Are you really okay with this?" Horikita stopped Ichinose, seeking confirmation yet again, just in case.

"Of course," answered Ichinose, without any hesitation. "Thank you for worrying about me. And Ayanokouji-kun, thank you too, for coming out so late."

"It's nothing. I just tagged along."

Ichinose bid us goodnight and then left. Horikita didn't stop her this time.

"I wonder if we really shouldn't do anything?" she said aloud.

"Who knows?" I replied.

Based on what we'd just seen, Ichinose seemed no different than usual. If I had to describe it, I wouldn't say she was acting tough, but more that she was trying not to think about the situation. That was my impression, anyway.

"What do you think I should do?" asked Horikita.

"You want my opinion?"

"Yes. I want your honest opinion," she replied without hesitation.

"In that case, I say do nothing."

"And your reasoning?"

"If Sakayanagi is the source of the rumors, as Ichinose said, then getting involved might cause her to set her sights on Class C."

"I see. But, what if Ichinose-san is defeated by Sakayanagi-san? Wouldn't Sakayanagi make Class C her next target, anyway?"

A natural conclusion. "It's certainly true we'll be targeted sooner or later. But when that time comes, the pesky leader of Class B will have already been dealt with. That'll work to our advantage."

"...So, you're saying you don't care about whatever happens to Ichinose-san? You're quite cold-blooded."

"Cold-blooded? Isn't that also how you acted at first? Helping a classmate is one thing, but Ichinose is from another class. She's an opponent we'll have to face. Her defeat would be a welcome development for us. There's no reason for us to lament it."

"She's currently our ally. Until Sakayanagi-san and the rest of Class A falls, and things come down to a one-on-one battle with Class B—"

"That's being pretty idealistic though, isn't it?" I said, interrupting her.

Class A being conveniently demoted to C, while Ichinose and Class C rose to A and B respectively, ending in us duking it out? That was nothing more than a pipe dream. While I wasn't sure how much she could really rely on other people in this situation, Ichinose was turning down people's offers to help her. If Horikita and Ichinose had had this conversation weeks ago, I was sure Horikita would have been satisfied and stopped offering help at a much earlier stage. How and why had she come to think the way she did now?

Well, I supposed I could hazard a guess. She *had* been striving to improve her relationship with Kushida, after all.

"You should leave things alone," I told her.

"I-I suppose..." Horikita didn't try to argue any further, which told me that she knew, deep down, that this was the right thing to do.

We'd been able to express to Ichinose that we were concerned about her, as a partner in our alliance, and that we were prepared to help. That was a good thing. Class C's best plan of action from here was to keep a low profile and ingratiate itself with the other classes, slowly closing in while they were busy battling each other. Here and now, it was important that we not seek to help them.

I'd given Horikita my opinion because she asked for it. It was ultimately up to her to decide what Class C did next, though I did think she probably wouldn't get further involved in what was going on with Class B. After all, she didn't have a way to really help improve the situation without getting in the way of Ichinose's plan.

"I'll head back too. A guy shouldn't be sticking around too long in a girl's room," I told her. If I stuck around past eight o'clock, there might be trouble.

"I suppose..." replied Horikita, lost in thought, without looking my way.

Horikita had begun to change, little by little. However, the changes she was going through were a little extreme. She was showing an increasing tendency to lose sight of her goals and be influenced by her surroundings. I imagined she'd keep struggling, both for her own sake and for others, for the foreseeable future. But would she move past that and finally become her true self? That was the most important thing.

After I left the room, I saw Ichinose standing in front of the elevator. While I wondered whether she had been waiting for me to come over, she waved at me with a broad smile on her face.

"Hey, over here!" she said in a quiet voice, calling me over.

I got onto the elevator, feeling like she was urging me on. She pushed the button for the first floor, sending us down to the lobby.

"Do you mind coming with me for a minute?" asked Ichinose.

"I don't mind, no, but... Where are we going?"

"Hm, would it be okay if we headed outside for a bit?"

We got to the lobby. Even though there wasn't anyone else around, we headed outside. The sun had set, and it was now completely dark. In that darkness, Ichinose and I walked over to one of the rest areas on the path toward the school building.

"I know that it's cold outside, but...I don't want to attract any attention."

"I understand. Are you okay, Ichinose?"

"I'm fine. Ah... Um, well, how do I say this... I'm really sorry."

I had wondered what she was going to say, but the first thing that came out of Ichinose's mouth was an apology.

"Why are you apologizing?" I asked.

"I guess since I've been causing problems for you and Horikita-san, Ayanokouji-kun, and the rest of Class C. I've caused you a lot of unnecessary worry because of these rumors. Please don't pay them any mind," said Ichinose.

"That's what you said to Kanzaki and the others, isn't it?"

"It's the best answer I have, I think. This is the stance I'm going to take until the rumors have gone away." Ichinose looked at me with determination in her eyes. If she'd addressed them this way, it was no wonder Kanzaki and the rest of her supporters in Class B had had no choice but to listen. "Well, that's all I had wanted to say... It really is cold, isn't it? Let's head on back."

"Okay."

We'd talked for just a moment. Ichinose had urged me to head inside first, so I made it back to the dorm before her.

4.5

THE DAILY LIVES of the people around me had gotten quite hectic. I hadn't even done anything particularly proactively myself, and I kept getting swept up in the things going on around me. Despite the ups and downs, maybe this *was* the kind of normal, everyday life that I'd wanted to have?

I had a hunch I was going to arrive at an answer—soon.

But then something strange happened.

The phone I'd placed near my bedside vibrated quietly. The clock showed that it was just past one in the morning. I checked to see who would be calling me at such an unusual time, but it was an unregistered number.

It shouldn't be possible for an outside number to contact me. The phones the school had provided us were only able to make and receive calls from school numbers, and there seemed to be no way to change those settings—a countermeasure put in place to prevent students from inadvertently making contact with the outside world. It wasn't a particularly unusual feature for a phone to have. There were similar parental controls you could activate when giving a phone to a small child, for instance.

In other words, the call was coming from someone on the school campus whose number hadn't been registered in my phone. I couldn't determine if it was from a student or from a teacher.

"...Hello?"

Still slightly sleepy, I cautiously answered the phone, pressing it to my left ear. No one spoke on the other end. The only sound that reached my ears was the faint sound of someone breathing.

We both waited in silence for about 30 seconds, as I waited for the other person to speak up.

"If you're not going to say anything, I'm hanging up," I said, warning the person on the other side that I had enough of waiting in silence.

"Ayanokouji Kiyotaka."

The person on the other side said my name. It was a male voice that I didn't remember ever hearing before, but it didn't sound like an adult. In which case, it was highly likely they were a student.

"And you are?" I asked in return.

The person went quiet again. And then, they hung up.

"Calling me just to say my name." I couldn't dismiss this as a simple wrong number. "So you've made your move, huh...?"

The identity of the caller was a trivial concern. I began to see that man's strategy. He'd begun moving against me. But why do this, and let me know he was coming? If his goal was to get me kicked out of school, then a surprise attack made more sense.

Deliberately doing something like this was a threat. A threat that he meant to crush me.

Was there anything at all that lay beyond that man's power...?

Regardless, there was no changing what had just begun.

5 ICHINOSE'S SECRET, KAMURO'S SECRET

TODAY WAS FRIDAY. Four days since Kanzaki had made contact with Hashimoto. The rumors about Ichinose had spread further with each passing day, to the point where it was no exaggeration to say the whole school knew of them. However, Ichinose had yet to report anything to the school. She seemed to pay the rumors no mind, going about her business as if nothing had changed. She stood firm in the face of the harassment.

People were beginning to speak up in support of her, saying things like "Rumors are just rumors, after all." These were all red herrings. They were nothing but lies.

Rumors didn't last forever, though.

The plan to defame Ichinose had ended in failure. She'd made it through the ordeal by maintaining her silence. As more and more people began to see it that way, their attention shifted to studying in earnest for the year-end final exams.

But something else happened during that time. Something that stoked the rumor mill again and caused fresh gossip to spread.

When I made it back to the dorm after class on Friday, I witnessed a large group of people gathered in the lobby. This was a familiar spectacle.

"Déjà vu, huh?"

Coincidentally, Katsuragi was standing in the same spot as last time. The difference this time was that Yahiko was standing next to him. Since there didn't seem to be anyone else around who I could talk to, I decided to approach Katsuragi and call out to him.

"What's all this fuss about?" I asked.

"Seems like there was a letter put in people's mailboxes. It's similar to the previous incident," muttered Katsuragi, crossing his arms in apparent disapproval.

"Didn't you get one too?" said Yahiko, directing his question at me at me a slight nod.

"I'll go check."

I went over to my mailbox, turned the dial of the combination lock, and checked the contents. I saw a piece of paper that had been carefully folded into fourths and placed inside. Just like before.

If this really was the same as last time, then it should be a printout. Of course, when a piece of paper was folded this many times, it made it harder to tell whether it was handwritten or printed.

I slowly unfolded the paper.

"Ichinose Honami is a criminal."

That was all it said. But this time around, the name of the sender wasn't included. It was also typed in a standard font, making it look exceedingly simple. Since I couldn't imagine this being printed at the convenience store, the sender had probably used a printer that they'd purchased themselves.

The sentence brought to mind those rumors that had just begun to die down. But the message was different this time. It simply said that she was a "criminal." No mention of *what* crimes she'd committed.

"I'm sure Ichinose must be exasperated by this prank."

"But won't saying it so blatantly cause a lot of problems? I mean, doing something this malicious more than once. That's going to cause trouble, isn't it?" asked Yahiko.

"The situation is certainly completely different from last time. The last letter merely hinted at the possibility that Ichinose had amassed points illegally. Although she was determined to have done nothing fraudulent, the school did recognize that she had a large number of points, so they made an unprecedented announcement recognizing their legitimacy. This time around, however, the contents of the letter are clearly designed to defame Ichinose. If we report this to the school and ask them to take action, there's a possibility they can identify the sender."

"Wow. Whoever sent it sure is an idiot, then."

"Well, I'm not so sure I would say that."

"Why's that?"

"I think the culprit would be well aware of something as simple as that."

"Huh…? Wait, you wouldn't happen to know who's been spreading those rumors, would you, Katsuragi-san?"

"Nothing more than a hunch is all."

Even though Sakayanagi had told me of her plans in advance, she publicly denied the truth of her involvement. It was possible Hashimoto had been working alone on this, or that he was acting on the orders of the second- or third-years. It was also possible that an entirely different person was the source of the rumors.

However, Katsuragi said he had a hunch about who the source might be. That meant Sakayanagi was obviously the clear candidate, right?

"Whether or not the school takes action will likely depend on the affected person: Ichinose."

The person who'd sent these letters was convinced Ichinose wouldn't report anything to the school, just like with the rumors of last time. They were confident that, no matter what they did, Ichinose would remain silent. If she took no action in response to the rumors or this letter, then the school couldn't act in response to her.

While all this went on, Ichinose had arrived at the dorm. No—it looked like she'd been contacted by her friends in Class B and then hurried back to the dorm. A friend handed her one of the letters right away, and she began to read it. Katsuragi, I, and the other ten or so students present watched her.

"............"

Ichinose didn't say anything. She just stood there, staring at the paper. It took no more than a second to read the statement on the paper, but she stared at the words, seeming to read them over and over, for dozens of seconds.

"...This was put in the mailboxes?"

"Yeah... It's awful, isn't it? It's probably in every first-year student's..."

One of the girls from Class B, Asakura Mako, approached Ichinose and hugged her.

"Hey, look, there's really no need to stand for this anymore. Why don't we talk to the teachers? This is unforgivable."

"Yeah, that's right. If we talk to the teachers, I'm sure they can find out who's behind this!"

Until now, there had just been unseen rumors. But this was different. This was a physical piece of evidence—clear proof that someone was attacking Ichinose with malicious intent.

"Don't worry. Something like this doesn't bother me," said Ichinose.

"B-but we have to do something! If we don't, these horrible rumors about you will just keep spreading, Honami-chan!"

It was no surprise that Ichinose's classmates were desperately trying to persuade her to act. Even if nine out of ten people dismissed the rumors, that one person who believed them would be all it took to make Ichinose Honami's reputation slowly deteriorate. Ichinose was un-hesitatingly committed to keeping her silence, but those around her felt differently. They were all looking for a way to help her, to prove that she was innocent, and to punish the culprit. Their attempts, however, would only back Ichinose further up against the wall.

"I'm sorry, everyone. For making you all worry about me. But really, please don't worry about this," said Ichinose, smiling at the girls of Class B.

There was almost no doubt that these letters had been distributed in the middle of the night, while everyone slept. Since no one really checked their mail first thing in the morning, the letters weren't discovered until after students returned to the dorms after class. All that remained, after that, was to wait for someone to find the letter and tell Ichinose about it.

There was one girl who carefully observed the upset girls from Class B. Katsuragi was glaring at her with a sharp gleam in his eyes. It was Kamuro Masumi, from first-year Class A. She was usually seen with Sakayanagi, but today, she seemed to be alone.

"Is something up with Kamuro?"

"No... It's nothing."

Katsuragi didn't give an answer. He tossed the letter away in a nearby trash bin and then pressed the button for the elevator. His face remained stern from the time he called the elevator until he and Yahiko finally boarded it, after it had come down from the first floor. As I watched the elevator go back up, I decided to return to my room.

5.1

MY ROOM WAS on the fourth floor of the dormitory: Room 401. When I got onto the elevator, Kamuro got on at the same time.

"What floor?" I asked her from my position right in front of the elevator buttons, but she didn't answer. Instead, she stood there in silence until the door closed. The elevator quietly began to move, bringing us to the fourth floor, where I disembarked. Kamuro exited right after me, like she was following me.

A simple coincidence? She was probably on her way to meet up with some guy. I walked to my door, and a second later, called out to Kamuro.

"Was there something you wanted?" I asked.

"I have something to talk to you about."

"I would have preferred it if you had said something sooner."

"What, do you have plans?"

"No. Is there any problem if we stand here and talk?" I asked.

"I catch cold pretty easily. If you don't mind, can you invite me in?" she asked.

If you don't mind, she said, but the request sounded almost like a threat.

"Sure, I don't mind..." I replied, unlocking the door and heading inside.

Kamuro ran her eyes across my room, her expression never changing. "Such a plain room."

"That's the first thing you say after forcing your way inside my room?" I asked.

"How did I force my way in? You gave me permission to enter, didn't you?" replied Kamuro, sitting down on my bed.

"Well, it was the way you got permission... Never mind. So what is it?"

"Get me something to drink. This is going to be a bit of a long story."

Wow, okay. She was pretty brazen. "Okay. I'll go make some tea or coffee."

"You don't have cocoa?" Unexpectedly, she requested a third option.

"...I do. Okay, cocoa it is, then."

I broached the subject of the talk she'd requested while I prepared the cocoa.

"So what did you want to talk about? If you're worried about the cold, we could've talked in the lobby." The lobby was heated, after all.

"No one will bother us here. This is the best place to talk."

"What do you want to talk about then?" I asked again. To be honest, I wasn't interested, and didn't particularly want to hear it.

"Are you getting defensive now?"

"It would be strange if I didn't. A girl whom I'm not close to—who's an enemy student from Class A, on top of that—just came into my room."

"Wow, you sure are quite different from Yamauchi," said Kamuro, still staring at me. Like she was testing me. "Aren't you curious?"

"Nope."

"Okay. Then I won't touch on that subject anymore. Whatever. It doesn't matter."

While Kamuro might be hiding a trick up her sleeve, like recording our conversation with her phone or a tape recorder, it was also true that her position was somewhat unique. Since Sakayanagi already knew about me, Kamuro didn't need to choose her words as carefully. Sakayanagi could attack me at any time, if she deemed it necessary. The reason she wasn't doing so right now was because she didn't want to draw attention to me.

"That letter earlier, about Ichinose," Kamuro asked. "What do you think about it?"

"What do you mean, what do I think?"

"Exactly what I said. Do you believe that she's a criminal, like the letter said?"

"Who knows? I'm not interested, anyway."

"Even if you're not interested, you must have an opinion on the matter. Do you think Ichinose is a good person or a bad person?" asked Kamuro.

"You can't say someone's a bad person just because they're a criminal, or that they're a good person just because they aren't." Good and bad were abstract concepts. How people defined them could vary greatly, depending on perspectives, positions, and relationships.

"........."

Kamuro stared at me, completely unamused. She didn't seem to want to let the conversation go in that direction at all. There was probably no way for me to avoid getting the heart of the matter any longer.

"I think it's connected to those rumors someone's been spreading," I said.

"I suppose so. I did hear about those rumors that have been going around."

"This is just conjecture on my part, but I think that one or more of those rumors might be true or at least somewhat close to being true. Which is exactly why Ichinose isn't fighting back against the rumors and against the letter. That's because if she did fight back, then the truth that she had been keeping hidden would be exposed," I reasoned.

"So, she thinks that if she continues to ignore them, the rumors will end up as nothing more than suspicions."

"Yeah. But that doesn't solve the problem. Ultimately, if the person who's spreading these rumors knows the real truth and keeps at it, they can get more and more specific with the rumors, without actually saying it themselves. When they do that, there's a high probability that Ichinose won't be able to hide it anymore."

The water came to a boil, and I poured it into a cup. Then, I put a cup of cocoa on the table. Kamuro didn't go to drink it right away.

"Not going to drink it?" I asked.

"I have a sensitive tongue."

I wondered how true that was.

"It's just as you've guessed. Right now, Ichinose is being targeted by a student who knows the truth that she wants to keep hidden."

"And how do you know that?" I asked.

"You know why. Sakayanagi said it right in front of you, after all."

I did remember that, of course. However, Kamuro didn't have any reason to tell me that herself. Was this also one of Sakayanagi's strategies?

"Just for your information, Sakayanagi doesn't know that I'm here talking to you right now. She'd probably be angry if she knew."

"So, this means that you're betraying Sakayanagi?"

"Yeah, it does."

"Sorry, but I can't really believe that."

"I figured. So I'll tell you the truth that Ichinose has been hiding. Besides, I'm sure that tomorrow or the day after, everyone will know it anyway."

So then, that means you can prove to me what you're saying is true then, huh?

"But before I tell you, there's something else. About why I'm being pushed around by Sakayanagi. That's something I need to tell you about."

"Your own personal story?"

"I know you're not interested, but just listen."

If it didn't matter whether or not I was interested. If all I had to do was listen, then I'll just listen. If I didn't do that, then she probably wasn't going to leave.

5.2

SAKAYANAGI HAD MADE CONTACT with me a week after the entrance ceremony. I'd stopped at a convenience store on my way back to my dorm, and finishing up my business there, had just left the store when one of my female classmates called out to me.

"Please wait a moment."

I stopped in my tracks. "What do you want?"

"Well, it hasn't been long since we started school here. I was just thinking I'd like to speak with you a bit, Kamuro-san."

"You remember my name, huh?"

"I made sure to memorize the names and faces of my classmates," the girl replied as she walked towards me. She moved at a slow pace. The cane that she gripped with one hand made it clear her legs weren't in the best shape.

If I'd remembered correctly, her name was...Sakayanagi Arisu, I think. Her physical handicap made her stand out. I made no real effort to memorize my classmates' names, but for some reason, hers stuck in my memory.

"Would you mind if we walked back to the dormitory together?" she asked.

I should've declined—but I didn't. It wasn't because her legs were bad. There was just something about the mood, in the moment, that made it difficult for me to turn her down.

"Sure, if you want."

"Thank you very much." Sakayanagi smiled happily. She sped up a bit to match my pace, walking beside me.

"I'm not going to help you if you push yourself too hard and fall over," I told her.

"Don't worry. My cane and I are quite well acquainted. We've been together a long time."

So she said, but...she was still moving pretty slowly. I intentionally released a heavy sigh. Which didn't seem to bother Sakayanagi at all. She might look frail at first glance, but apparently, she was quite bold on the inside.

"By the way...what were you doing at the convenience store, earlier?" she asked.

"What do you mean?"

"It doesn't look like you purchased anything."

"What does it matter? There wasn't anything I wanted."

I tried to bring the conversation to a close, but Sakayanagi grabbed hold of my arm.

"You shoplifted, didn't you?" she said, meeting my gaze squarely. Her eyes were sparkling, almost as if she'd found herself a fun new toy. "I'm assuming you already checked out the place several times, so you knew the positioning of the cameras. Was this your first time shoplifting at this school? How many times have you done it before?"

"You're really that certain I stole something?"

"Yes. It seems you aren't taking me very seriously, but yes, I am quite confident that you did. If I weren't, I wouldn't have asked you if you had shoplifted."

"I suppose you have a point." She'd called out to me precisely because she'd seen me there. "So even if I did steal something, then what? You gonna rat me out to the school or something?"

"Hm, let's see. While it would be a simple enough matter for me to report this incident, please listen to what I have to say first."

"Huh?"

Sakayanagi kept going, ignoring my scowl.

"Your execution was superb. What surprised me most of all, though, was how cool and composed you were. Most people would also buy something cheap, like gum or candy, to assuage their guilt. You did nothing of the sort, and I get the feeling you never have. More proof that the act of shoplifting has become something of a routine for you."

She was right on the money. Just from watching me do it once, she'd inferred that I'd done it many times before. But so what? What did that matter? I had no intention of drawing out this conversation. No matter how good my execution had been, the fact remained that she'd seen me.

"Do whatever you want," I told her.

I reached into my bag and pulled out the can of beer I'd stolen from the convenience store. People under twenty weren't allowed to buy alcohol. The shops only stocked it for the teachers and other staff living on campus.

"Just hurry up and contact them already," I added.

What Sakayanagi said next, however, was a complete non sequitur. "Do you often drink alcohol?"

"Huh? ...No. I'm not really interested in booze."

"So shoplifting isn't something you do to make your daily life easier. Rather, you do it just for the thrill, right?" said Sakayanagi, analyzing the situation. "For the feelings of guilt?"

"Okay, I get it, you can see right through me. So why don't you just hurry up and hand me over to the school already?"

"Are you sure that's what you want? If the school finds out you shoplifted, then suspension is quite likely, don't you think?"

"And?"

"It's only been one week since we started school. There are still so many things, both fun and not so fun, to look forward to, aren't there?"

"If you're not going to contact the school, I'll do it myself."

I moved to take out my phone, but she stopped my hand.

"I quite like you, Kamuro Masumi-san. You're going to be my very first friend," said Sakayanagi, urging me to put my phone away.

"What are you saying?"

"In exchange for keeping your secret, I'd like you to help me with a few things, please."

"That isn't what I'd call friendship."

"Oh, really?"

"Besides, do you think I'll just obediently do as you say?"

"It's certainly true that even if I report you, the penalties the school inflicts on you would likely be minimal. But the fact that you, Kamuro Masumi, are a shoplifter would become known to all. And that would make it hard for you to ever shoplift again, hm?"

"You're saying you won't just overlook me shoplifting this time, but you also don't care if I do it again?"

"Whatever you do is entirely up to you. I will do nothing to influence your actions. Besides, even if I tried to appeal to you from a moral standpoint, telling you such criminal acts are wrong, my words would have no lasting impact. Am I wrong?"

"Well, that's..."

"Regardless...I think that if you follow me, your life will be anything but boring. Perhaps I can help you scratch this itch that currently only shoplifting assuages, hm?"

That was my first encounter with Sakayanagi Arisu.

- -

" ...**A**H, MAN, I'm exhausted. It's been a long time since I talked that much."

Having finished her story, Kamuro gazes at me with the same look in her eyes that she had since we started the conversation.

"So basically, I'm a habitual shoplifter."

"Even recently?"

"Sakayanagi has been working me to the bone. I haven't had the time to shoplift."

Despite saying that, Kamuro didn't sound entirely dissatisfied. She'd probably never been *needed* by anyone before, which had led to the darkness she kept within in her heart. The fact that Sakayanagi now needed her kept her from continuing to commit crimes.

If that was the case, Sakayanagi was making good use of

her. If Kamuro kept shoplifting, sooner or later, she'd be caught. She might have flown under the radar if she were doing it off campus, but the school provided her a very limited territory to work in. If on-campus store owners noticed continuing inconsistencies in their inventory, then they'd quickly figure out the truth. And if that happened, Class A would take some significant damage.

"Sakayanagi said something at the school camp about you and Ichinose sharing the same secret," I told her. In other words, if I assumed Kamuro was telling me the truth, it meant Ichinose has a history of shoplifting too.

"Exactly."

"So what exactly do you hope to achieve by telling me the truth about your past?" Depending on the circumstances, I might be able to use this to investigate her past. If that happened, Kamuro would be the only one losing out.

"I don't particularly like Sakayanagi or Ichinose or anything. But it's just that, well, the truth about Ichinose shoplifting really was a shock to me, honestly. She's so popular. You'd think she would be satisfied with everything she has, but she's actually the same as me." Kamuro chuckled self-deprecatingly. "Stop Sakayanagi. You can do it, can't you?"

"In other words, you're asking me to save Ichinose?" I asked.

"Yes. If things keep going this way, Ichinose is going to be crushed, and I don't mean physically. I mean her heart."

"I see."

It was difficult to verify the truth of Kamuro's story. A store owner could detect monetary discrepancies or missing items by thoroughly analyzing their inventory, but that wouldn't tell them the cause of the missing items. The loss could be the result of an employee's processing error.

Kamuro had said that she'd shoplifted when she started school here, but she obviously didn't just steal the same items over and over again. I could hardly ask the store to show me their surveillance camera footage. The only thing I *could* do was leak the fact of Kamuro's shoplifting to the school and to the convenience store employees, but irrespective of the truth of her story, that posed far too much of a personal risk to me.

Even if everything she said was true, I wasn't inclined to take her words at face value. While it was probably true that she was dissatisfied with Sakayanagi, that was hardly enough incentive to make her come looking to me, a complete unknown, for help.

What was the point of this sequence of events, then? Realistically speaking, should I assume this was all happening at Sakayanagi's command? She might be using Ichinose to set up a direct confrontation with me.

"You think that I'm lying?" asked Kamuro, breaking the silence after a long period of consideration.

"To be honest, there's no guarantee what you said is true," I told her.

Of course, based on what she'd told me, I'd come to the conclusion that it almost certainly *was* true. Even so, her close connection with Sakayanagi made me wary of admitting that.

"...I see. In that case, how about I prove it to you?"

"Can you prove it?"

"Probably." Kamuro took out her student ID and handed it to me. "Okay, then. Wait for me, and don't lock your door."

With that, she left the room. Wait a minute... Was she really planning on stealing something right now to prove she was a shoplifter?

I idly examined Kamuro's student ID while I waited. About 10 minutes later, she returned. She took something out from under her clothes and showed it to me.

"Hey, hey..."

It seemed I'd guessed correctly.

"I thought about taking some gum or something, but figured a beer would give my story more credibility," said Kamuro.

True enough. Anyone could buy gum. She could have just purchased it in advance and pretended to have stolen it. Alcohol was a different story. Even if she borrowed another student's ID, she couldn't have purchased an alcoholic beverage. It was impossible for students to purchase age-restricted goods.

Additionally, it was extremely unlikely that a teacher or one of the employees working on campus could have gotten it for her. There was no mistaking the fact that this was stolen merchandise. Had she done this in order to gain my trust?

"Get it now?" Kamuro moved to put the can of beer away, but I reached out my hand.

"Just in case, I want to verify that it's the real deal. It could be fake."

"...Moron. You really think I could fake something like this?"

Kamuro seemed reluctant for a moment but then quickly handed over the can. It was ice-cold, which made me think that it had just come from the convenience store. I gently looked over the can, rotating it slowly. It was most certainly a real alcoholic beverage.

"If you really want, you can just have it, you know?"

"No thanks." In the unlikely event something like this was discovered in my room, it would spell trouble for me.

"Yeah, I suppose," Kamuro took the can back. She tapped lightly on it with her hands and repeatedly tossed it in the air and caught it, over and over. "So, anyway, do you believe me?"

"You showed me the real thing. I can't not believe you now."

"I'm glad to hear that."

"So why me?" I asked.

"You're the only person in this school who I can come to. You should know that much," said Kamuro.

I picked up the cup of cocoa I had prepared for Kamuro, since I was sure she wasn't going to drink it. Ten minutes had passed without her taking a sip, and it had gotten cold.

"I stand to gain nothing from this," I told her.

"Probably not, no," said Kamuro. She stood up, seemingly satisfied. "I'm looking forward to seeing how this ends."

As if trying to bring the conversation to a close, she moved to leave the room.

"Wait a second."

"...What?"

"You forgot your student ID."

Kamuro grabbed it with her free hand—her other still holding the can of beer—and left.

All things considered, this really raised some troublesome questions for me. Was ignoring everything going on with Ichinose the best plan of action, after all?

"Well... I suppose I can't know that for sure, can I?" I said aloud.

In fact, it might be best to take advantage of this opportunity.

I grabbed my student ID and my phone, left my room, and made my way to the convenience store. While I was on the way there, I got a call from Horikita's brother. I'd thought I finally had a chance to relax, now that my guest had left, but...

Well, this was a call from a rather unexpected person. I doubted he was calling just to chat.

"There are a few things I'd like to talk to you about," said Horikita when I answered the call.

"Is this urgent?" I asked.

"Depending on how things play out, it might be too late. It's about my sister."

"...About your sister?"

This was unexpected too. Horikita's brother wouldn't be talking about his sister unless there was something serious going on.

"Kushida Kikyou contacted Nagumo Miyabi."

"Huh?" I was surprised, but also impressed by the speed at which the news had reached Horikita's brother. "And here I thought you were surrounded by enemies on all sides. You've acquired some good information. Who did you get it from?"

"From Kiriyama. It's clear from what happened at the school camp that my relationship with Nagumo has fractured significantly. I'm almost certain he'll be launching an attack before long. I have no choice but to make a move myself," said Horikita.

Vice President Kiriyama, huh. While I thought things over in silence, Horikita continued speaking.

"You don't trust him at all, do you?" he asked.

"That's because I don't know Kiriyama as well as you do," I told him.

"That's all right. You always err on the side of caution."

As the man serving as student council president, Horikita always approached others with a certain degree of trust, whether it be Kiriyama or Nagumo. Even if he had his suspicions, he gave them the benefit of the doubt until he was actually betrayed. That was something I could never do.

"So what's up?"

"She asked Nagumo for help in getting Suzune expelled. Quite a bold move."

"I see she's acting out with no regard for appearances or consequences, then."

Kushida, after losing her wager with Horikita, had said she wouldn't do anything to interfere in the future.

This proved she had no intention of honoring her promise. She'd tried to use Ryuuen to her advantage in the past, and now she'd approached Nagumo. Assuming she'd seen what Nagumo did at the school camp, it wasn't a surprising thing for her to do, really.

Of course, Kushida had to realize what this meant. That every time she pushed against Horikita like this, she was also driving herself further into the corner. But as they said, no pain, no gain. You could really sense her determination.

To be honest, while it might have been premature for her to reach out to Ryuuen when she did, it wasn't a bad idea for her to rub elbows with Nagumo. Working with a senior one year above her meant that once he graduated and was out of the picture, there would be no one around who knew what had happened. But that only held true if Nagumo was someone she could trust.

"I anticipate Nagumo, or someone close to him, will strike Suzune in the near future," said Horikita.

"So what do you want me to do? Protect your little sister?" I asked.

"If Suzune ends up getting expelled from school, that will be her own fault. However, Kushida also named you as someone who has caused her trouble."

"I see..."

Nagumo might not have been too interested in me,

but if my name kept coming up like this, then it was going to stick in his memory whether he wanted it to or not. If I didn't do something to sever this connection sooner rather than later, the problems it caused would just keep mounting.

"Is it possible that Nagumo and Hashimoto have been in contact?" I asked.

"Why are you asking that?"

"I thought I noticed a slight change in Hashimoto's behavior between the start of the school camp and the end. I wasn't sure of what I was seeing, but when I saw him the other day, I became certain it wasn't just my imagination. I suspect someone told Hashimoto something about me during our time at the school camp," I answered.

The number of students who'd taken notice of me and could pass that information onto Hashimoto were extremely limited, to say the least.

"It's just as you suspected. Nagumo warned Hashimoto about you during the school camp. That being said, Hashimoto still probably hasn't arrived at the conclusion that you are the student manipulating Suzune."

"I see." Which meant he was sniffing around to try to ascertain the truth of the matter himself.

"I didn't think I'd really need to come right out and ask you this, but are you displeased?"

"No. Even if you'd told me beforehand, it wouldn't change the current situation," I replied.

Horikita muttered an "I suppose so" in response.

I didn't care if a student from Sakayanagi's faction distrusted me. No matter how hard they tried to investigate me, as long as I did nothing, they'd come up empty. Even if they did come up with a strategy of their own, the moment they shared it with Sakayanagi, that would be the end of it. In that sense, she was easier to deal with Ryuuen or Nagumo.

Of course, Nagumo was at the center of all of this. Which meant just standing by and observing might cause me problems down the line too.

"I've given you information. What you do with it is your decision," said Horikita.

"I suppose so."

The call was disconnected.

In a school like this, information of the sort that the elder Horikita had just given me was useful in more than a few ways. Not a day passed in this school without someone enacting schemes to entrap someone else, which made Horikita's brother a useful source of information. While he wasn't as dexterous as Nagumo, and his information network wasn't as extensive, he was far more credible and accurate.

Regardless, it seemed the first sparks were already starting to fly. I probably needed to move fast if I was going to stop this from becoming a full-blown fire.

6 RUMORS RUNNING RAMPANT

THE WEEKEND WAS OVER, and Monday was here. I took my morning shower and then brushed my teeth while drying my hair off with a towel. My plan was to take things slower than usual, lingering in my room as long as possible without actually being late to class.

I'd slept with my phone turned off last night. I turned it back on now and saw some messages immediately light up my screen.

Kiyotaka-kun, do you have a little time this morning? Can I come to your room?

It was a message from Airi, apparently sent right after I stepped in the shower. I saw a missed call from Kei too, but I'd just call her back later.

Sorry, I was taking a shower and didn't see your message.

I don't really have time now. Can we meet at school? I texted back. Less than a second later, I saw that she'd read it. Was that just a coincidence? Or was she waiting for me to respond?

That's okay, don't worry about it. I'll talk to you later, replied Airi, making me think it must not have been an urgent matter.

I decided to focus on getting ready for now. I was out of time to laze about, so I finished getting dressed and headed over to take the elevator to the lobby. It was generally packed full of students on their way to school in the morning, making it slow to respond, but given how close I was cutting it, it shouldn't be too busy now.

I pushed the button to summon the elevator, then took out my phone and sent a message to Kei.

What did you want? If it's possible, I'd like to meet you sometime today this evening or later tonight to talk.

The message was marked as read almost immediately.

Kei texted back. *I wasn't calling for any reason in particular, so no worries. Anyway, I'm okay with meeting up, but can we do it earlier? I have plans to hang out with my friends tonight.*

How about five o'clock? I suggested. *Six would be okay too.*

Okay, let's do five then, please. What is it about?

Let's talk when we meet.

The elevator came down from the upper floors just as I sent that last reply. Hirata was the only one inside.

"Oh, good morning, Ayanokouji-kun," he said.

"This is a rare sight, Hirata. You're cutting it pretty close today too, huh?"

Hirata was an honors student, so he almost always made it to class with plenty of time to spare. It was pretty unusual for him to be leaving the dormitory late, let alone at the last possible minute, like this.

"Well, I had really planned on leaving earlier, but..." said Hirata, a bitter smile on his face, looking somewhat conflicted.

That was vague. "But?"

As we made it to the lobby and got off the elevator, I saw several girls awaiting us. Not girls from just one class either, but girls from all four—from A to D. I wondered for a moment why they were all gathered here like this, but then immediately realized what was going on.

"Good morning, Hirata-kun!"

"Oh, good morning." While Hirata wore a charming smile, he still seemed a little out of sorts.

"This...is a valentine, for you!"

All six girls presented him with chocolates at the same time. I had to imagine this precise scenario had been repeated many times this morning, forcing Hirata to keep going back to his room to drop off chocolates.

I said a hasty goodbye and hurried off to class. I could've waited for him, but I was overwhelmed by the pressure I was feeling from the girls, who were emanating a clear vibe of "You're in the way."

That was right. It was Valentine's Day, wasn't it?

"I've never gotten chocolates before..." I muttered to myself without meaning to.

I kind of wanted to be given chocolates before I did something like get a girlfriend, which surprised me, to tell the truth. I hadn't thought I was capable of wanting such things, even faintly.

6.1

I WASN'T THE ONLY GUY who was excited about Valentine's Day. As soon as I arrived at Class C, I felt the classroom enveloped in a strange atmosphere. Many of the guys were clustered together in one place. Today was the culmination of an entire year of hard work. Just like Christmas, this was an event that put a spotlight on lovers.

"Oh, you showed up, huh, Ayanokouji? Come over here for a sec," said Sudou.

I went over to him.

"Did you get any chocolate?" he asked, his face tense, like he was really pressing me for an answer. He was almost glaring at me.

"Huh?"

"Let me translate that for you. It seems like he's actually asking, 'Did you get any chocolate *from Horikita?*'" said Ike, with a grin.

"Don't go running your mouth, idiot. Ain't got nothin' to do with this," said Sudou, not smiling at all. If anything, his eyes were filled with this almost demonic energy, like he was saying, 'Well?'

"I didn't get any. There's no way I would," I answered.

"...Really?" asked Sudou.

"Yeah."

Sudou nodded a couple times in response, then released me from his piercing glare.

"Well, I get why Ken's all panicky. I mean, Ayanokouji's *thing* is a total monster, after all," said Ike, drawing the outline of something like a plastic bottle in the air with his hand as he spoke.

"...Okay Ayanokouji, don't think you've won just because you've got *that*, okay?" said Sudou.

"No, I don't think that at all..."

I'd been occasionally getting comments like that since the school camp, and it was honestly beginning to annoy me.

"Come to think of it, how are you doing, Kanji? Things going well with Shinohara?"

"H-huh? Why you bringin' up Shinohara?"

"Come on, dude, enough already. Just be straight with us. Everyone already knows already."

"E-everyone... knows?" said Ike, directing his question at me for some reason. I more or less got where the conversation was going, so I nodded lightly in response.

"Ugghhh!" Ike immediately crouched down, his face turning red.

"See? Even a total recluse like Ayanokouji knows about it. So did you get any chocolates?" asked Sudou.

Perhaps because Shinohara wasn't really all that popular in our class, I didn't hear anyone around us commenting that they were jealous of Ike. I'd expected Yamauchi, his usual partner in crime, to razz him and be resentful, but he was nowhere to be seen.

"I didn't get anythin'..." replied Ike.

"Guess you and I are the same, then," said Sudou. He gave Ike a sympathetic pat on the shoulder.

"W-well, it doesn't matter anyway. 'Cause I got some from Kushida-chan," said Ike, proudly showing off a box of chocolates with a pink ribbon on it.

"Uh, okay, dude, you say that, but didn't every guy in class get some? I did too," said Sudou.

"I'm still grateful, but yeah, I guess it really is just obligation chocolate at best."

I'd never expected Kushida would give chocolate to all

the first-year boys. I wondered how she'd done it? Well, I supposed it wasn't that usual, given this was Kushida we were talking about.

The air was charged with the guys' overwhelming enthusiasm. I couldn't help but feel like it was precisely this kind of childish behavior that made the girls keep their distance, but then again, my classmates had so little experience in the realm of love. This was inevitable, even if their desperation changed nothing. Your chances of getting chocolate depended on how you'd behaved in the days leading up to this, not how desperate you got now that the moment was here.

At least, that was the conclusion I came to as I watched a girl from Class B give Akito some chocolate.

"Tomorrow, on the 15th, we'll be having a comprehensive practice test covering all subjects, just as the schedule indicated. However, as I had said before, this will have no bearing on your grades. The purpose of this test is to, at most, measure your current abilities. In addition, it will serve as good practice for the year-end exams. Many of the questions on the practice test will be similar to what you'll see on the year-end test, though of course, they won't be exactly the same. Don't get careless just because you got promoted to Class C," said Chabashira.

That much appreciated explanation marked the end of today's lessons. I decided to say a few words to my neighbor as she was getting ready to leave.

"How are things with Kushida lately?" I asked.

"What do you mean?" replied Horikita.

"I mean, are things going well?"

"I don't know. I'm doing my utmost to come up with ways to improve our relationship. Are you considering helping me?"

"I'm just asking is all."

"Kushida-san has been changing, little by little," said Horikita.

"What do you mean, changing?"

"I'm going to go have tea with her at Keyaki Mall later today. Normally, she would have turned me down without a second thought," said Horikita.

Apparently, things were going better than I had thought—if only on the surface.

"So does that mean that your hopes are being realized?" I asked.

"If we talk to one another, we may be able to come to some mutual understanding."

"That would be good. Well, see ya." With that brief response, I got up from my seat.

"...Okay, what was that about?" said Horikita, shooting me a slightly contemptuous look. She rose from her seat too.

"Ah, Suzune. Uh, um... When would be a good time to get some help with my studies?" asked Sudou.

"My, you're being quite proactive, Sudou-kun," said Horikita.

"Well, I guess. I don't wanna get expelled, after all," said Sudou nervously. I was willing to bet his real goal was to get some Valentine's Day chocolate from Horikita. "Any time works for me today. So?"

However...

"Your club still hasn't gone on break yet, has it? I can help you study after the practice test. It won't be too late," replied Horikita, dashing Sudou's hopes to the ground as I left the classroom.

Someone shouted my name, the sound echoing throughout the hall. Well...I say "shouted'" but the actual volume of the words was quite low.

"Kiyotaka-kun!"

"What's up, Airi?" I asked.

"Is it really true that you're not meeting with the group today?"

"I wasn't planning to, no." The Ayanokouji Group had invited me to hang out, but I'd declined. I still had a problem that needed to be dealt with at the moment.

"I-I think it'll be okay even if you come later. Do you think you could still come?"

"Hmm... I might not be free until sometime after six. Is that okay?"

"Yeah! I think everyone should still be together by then!"

"All right. We'll, I'll get in touch later then, okay?" I answered.

That brief comment was enough to change Airi's stiff expression to a broad smile. I parted ways with her and got moving again.

When I made it to Class B, the classroom was strangely quiet. There were only a few students I really wanted to talk to—Kanzaki would have been my first choice, but Sumida or Moriyama, who'd been with me at the school camp, would do as well. Unfortunately, all three had left the classroom by the time I arrived.

I could probably have picked someone at random, but I wasn't going to do that. I turned around and left. On my way out, I overheard a shred of conversation between some Class B girls.

"Hey... Do you think the reason Honami-chan is absent today is because...?"

"No, there's no way."

So, Ichinose was absent, huh? As I walked away from Class B, I wondered if it was mere coincidence, or if it had something to do with what had happened the other day.

How had Sakayanagi come to know Ichinose's secret in the first place? Sure, there were conversational techniques like cold reading and hot reading that could be used to extract a person's secrets, but I couldn't imagine Ichinose willingly revealing her past as a shoplifter. Her refusal to comment on the rumors, even now, was proof of that. Would she really have let herself be coaxed into telling one of her greatest enemies, a member of Class A, such a secret? I mean, Ike and Yamauchi were one thing, but Ichinose was quite clever.

"Did she just succumb to Sakayanagi trying to wheedle it out of her...?" I asked myself aloud.

Or was there someone else who knew Ichinose's secret? But even Kanzaki, whom she probably trusted the most out of anyone in Class B, didn't seem to know it. I couldn't imagine her close friends knew it either, judging by their reactions. So maybe the teaching staff at school, or...the student council, which Ichinose was a part of.

"If Nagumo betrayed Ichinose and chose to side with Sakayanagi, then it's possible, I suppose," I reasoned.

This was a theory based on several assumptions, though. And besides, unless everything Kamuro had said was true, nothing could be substantiated. The only person who could overturn the premise of this assumption would be Ichinose Honami herself.

Though this school could be called huge, in the eyes of the rest of the world, the campus was actually a rather confined space. If you met with someone in secret, there was always the danger of being seen. That meant you usually had to meet either early in the morning or in the middle of the night to avoid detection.

I didn't know Ichinose Honami's room number, but that was easily fixed—I could just call the dormitory management office and ask for it. From the school's point of view, there was no reason to keep student room numbers secret. If you said that you were a student, and that you were trying to get in touch with each other, then the school should cooperate with you.

I called to confirm her room number while I walked and managed to get it right away. As I did so, I ignored Hashimoto, who was watching me from a distance. He'd been tailing me frequently in the afternoons and evenings of late, and he wasn't too shabby at it either. I could tell he'd had plenty of experience tailing people.

On the surface, it might seem like there was no merit to me doing something like visiting Ichinose while I was being watched. In fact, the opposite was true. It was precisely *because* I was being watched that the action was worthwhile. Besides, I wanted to confirm something with Ichinose.

I hurried back to the dorm and went to her floor. Unfortunately, there were several girls standing in front of her room when I arrived, all people whom Ichinose was particularly close to.

I quickly turned back around and got back on the elevator, deciding to call it a day for now.

6.3

FIVE O'CLOCK CAME, and I asked Kei to meet me at a spot that was a little ways away from the dorms. It wasn't exactly a well-populated location, but it wasn't as though no one ever came there either.

"Ah, it's so cold! Why are we meeting in a place like this, anyway? There are lots of other options, aren't there?" she complained.

"Well, we can't exactly meet in the lobby, can we? If we meet out in the open, people will start whispering about us, and that would be bad for you, wouldn't it?"

"Well, I suppose, but...doesn't meeting secretly like this actually make us look even more suspicious? If anyone sees us, there'll definitely be all kinds of rumors popping up..."

"Don't worry about it."

"You know, I kinda get the feeling that you're not being very cautious. But that's fine, I guess."

That was all right. After all, it would be a long wait for the guy who'd been following me.

"Still, it's way too cold out. I wish summer would hurry up and come already," said Kei.

"Aren't you going to just end up saying you wish winter would hurry up and come once summer does roll around?"

Kei pondered that for a bit, then sniffed. "That's just how a maiden's heart works," she answered, pouting a bit. "Come to think of it, I wonder if there's going to be a special exam this month?"

"Well, we only just got done with the school camp. It wouldn't surprise me if there's no special exam this month."

"So you think we can breathe easy for a bit?"

"Are you going to be all right for the year-end exam? It'll probably be pretty difficult." When I said that, Kei's posture grew stiff.

"Huh...? Seriously?" she said.

She'd managed to somehow squeak past in the exams we've had so far, but she couldn't afford to get careless with her studies.

"Help me study," said Kei.

"Ask Hirata... Actually, while I suppose that's not impossible, it might be pretty difficult, huh?"

Kei certainly was audacious enough to ask Hirata to tutor her if she felt like it, even after they'd just broken up. But she didn't seem to be too keen on the idea. She was staring at me. The easiest solution would be to have Keisei tutor her, but that wasn't realistic. If I tossed her into the midst of our group without warning, it would have repercussions.

"It would have to be in the middle of the night. Is that okay?" I asked.

"It's way better than getting expelled."

Well put. "All right, then. I'll go ahead and put together a schedule."

"Thanks."

Even if we got through the year-end exam, though, there'd be new problems on the horizon soon after. We could probably expect to see a massive special exam around the start of March. If we made it safely through that, we'd have completed our first year of school. The school would keep us fighting to the bitter end, so we couldn't afford to let our guards down.

"So, anyway, what did you need from me?" asked Kei, seeming a little fidgety and nervous for some reason.

"Something up?" I asked.

"No, not really. It's just...I was thinking it seemed like you really wanted to meet with me today, for some reason."

"I just had something I wanted to confirm. It would've been fine if we didn't get to it today."

"Hmph," she scoffed, shooting me a look of suspicion. Deciding to pay it no mind, I focused on the topic at hand.

"Any idea whose number this might be?" I asked, showing her the unregistered phone number that I had gotten a call from the other day.

"Huh? Who is that from? What, are you getting calls from strangers or something?"

"Seems that way."

Kei brought up her contacts and manually entered the number via the keypad. If the number was registered in her contacts, then the person's name and other information should show up.

"Doesn't seem like anything's coming up."

"I do have more contacts in my phone than the average girl, but I don't know most of the seniors," said Kei.

I'd hoped she'd get a hit after checking her contacts, giving me a new lead to investigate. But I supposed the odds of that happening were slim, after all.

"Why not just try calling the number back directly?" she asked.

"I've tried doing that several times, but whoever it is has their phone off."

"Hm...? If it's important, do you want me to look into it for you?"

"Sure. That was why I called you out here today, anyway. But don't do anything careless," I told her.

"Got it," answered Kei, nodding, taking note of the number. "Is that all?"

"Yep. See ya."

I tried to bring our conversation to a close, but Kei hurriedly moved to stop me, looking flustered.

"Oh, uh, by the way, um... there's something I kind of wanted to talk to you about. Can I ask you a question?" A strange question, as it turned out. "What day is today? Okay, 5, 4, 3—"

"...That's a much easier question than I expected. Actually, it's so easy that I'm worried I'm going to give you the wrong answer after all," I replied.

"Don't overthink it. Just give me a straight answer."

"Valen—"

"Yes, that is correct," she replied, cutting me off.

I felt my head being lightly bonked by a box.

"You're giving me this?" I asked.

"I got it for Yousuke-kun, but there's no need to give it to him anymore."

"For Hirata, huh?"

"What? You don't like it?"

"No, it's not that. I was just thinking that you must have prepared this quite a long while in advance," I replied. Kei had decided to break it off with Hirata already well over a month ago now.

"I-I prepare for things very thoroughly! Even though I decided I was going to break up with him, I thought it might still be useful to have, okay? Well, I guess it's not like I should expect someone like you, a complete beginner to the world of romance, to understand."

I supposed she had a point.

"I was just thinking that maybe you chose today to meet because you were hoping to get some chocolate from me," she added.

"Sorry. Didn't think about that at all," I replied.

Kei wore a look of irritation for a moment but then quickly recovered and changed the topic of conversation, like she was trying to avoid something. "By the way, did you get anything from other girls?"

"Nope, didn't get anything."

I'd decided beforehand to tell her that regardless of whether I actually received anything or not.

"Ha, too bad, so sad. Guess you're a guy with zero prospects, then," she replied, switching to making fun of me at the drop of a hat.

"Are you sure you want to give this to me, then? If you give it to me, that means I no longer have zero prospects, right?" I replied.

"That just makes it even more pathetic. That means you've gotta come to me for salvation." She was really condescending to me now. "Oh, by the way, feel free to return the favor by paying me back a thousand times over, if you like."

Well, that was just extremely absurd.

"By the way, um—"

Kei tried to change the subject yet again, but the words seemed to get stuck in her throat when she met my gaze. We stood close together, gazing into each other's eyes, until I slowly shifted my line of sight in the direction of the dormitory.

"Well, I'll head back to my room then," said Kei.

"Okay. See you."

Kei left for the dorms, and I put her present into my bag right away.

7 AMBIGUOUS THINGS

For hashimoto masayoshi, the question of who to follow was trivial. Actually, it wasn't an exaggeration to say that he didn't care at all. It didn't matter to him whether Sakayanagi or Katsuragi led Class A; he would simply use whoever served him best. That was all there was to it.

While he'd been fortunate enough to start out in Class A, he had considered the possibility of dropping down to Class B or Class C along the way. The important thing for him was to get into a position where he could turn the tables on his foes, whoever they were, and pull off a late-stage victory in the end. That was precisely why he'd made contact with Ryuuen Kakeru at an early stage in his rise to power, sensing his potential. Ryuuen was a person of exceptional talent, capable of defeating both

Sakayanagi and Ichinose. Hashimoto recognized his unsettling power.

If necessary, Hashimoto wouldn't hesitate to leak information about Class A to Ryuuen. Of course, he was currently conducting reconnaissance on Sakayanagi's behalf, at most. However, if Ryuuen ever did surpass the others, Hashimoto was prepared to betray Sakayanagi.

He'd also set his sights on Ichinose from Class B, in the same fashion. But Ichinose wasn't like Ryuuen and Sakayanagi. You couldn't engage her with shady, under-handed tactics. And so, rather than trying to force the issue, Hashimoto chose instead to remove the obstacles in the way of his objective.

He'd made contact with a girl in Class B who was close to Ichinose. He wasn't able to get her to go so far as to betray Ichinose, but the connection had been established at least, and he went on to establish similar relationships with people from each of the four classes. There was simply no such thing as having too much insurance against unexpected events.

And today, he was trying to make preliminary arrangements in preparation for one such "unexpected event."

"U-um, Hashimoto-kun, do you have a minute?"

One of Hashimoto's classmates, a girl named Motodoi Chikako, called out to him in the hallway after class. Like

Hashimoto, she was in the tennis club. Apparently, she'd run after him after he left the classroom. She looked nervous and fidgety.

Hashimoto immediately understood what was happening without her saying a word. Today was February 14th. He'd already experienced this sort of thing many times. Of course, even though he understood what was going on, he didn't let it show on his face. Nor did he say a word.

"What's up, Motodoi? Something you wanna talk to me about?" he asked gently.

At that, Motodoi seemed to gather the courage to come out with it. "Here, for you. Chocolate. Because it's Valentine's Day today," she replied, handing some chocolate to Hashimoto, which he immediately accepted.

"Thanks, Motodoi. This makes me really happy."

"I-I'm glad!"

Hashimoto had noticed some time ago that Motodoi had been looking at him fondly for a while now. The chocolate she'd just given him was undoubtedly an expression of romantic feelings. While he felt confident that she'd say yes if he asked her to go out with him, he felt nothing whatsoever for Motodoi in return.

For better or worse, he thought of her only as someone who wasn't worth using. He had already determined that there was absolutely zero benefit to going out with her.

"You should drop by the club every now and again," she added.

"Sorry. Guess I've been skipping all the time lately, huh?"

"Seriously! Our senpai are so totally exasperated."

"I'll remember that. Anyway, I'll make sure to thank you properly next month," Hashimoto said.

"O-okay."

Motodoi blushed, nodded, and then ran off, as if trying to escape her embarrassment. There was absolutely no chance that he'd go out with her, but Hashimoto still left the option open by hinting to her about it. Something might change in the future, after all.

He sped up his pace a bit as he made his way to first-year Class C, trying to make up for lost time. There was currently one person occupying far more of his attention than Motodoi, and it was a boy from Class C named Ayanokouji Kiyotaka.

"Why can't I stop thinking about him?" murmured Hashimoto. A part of him couldn't help but wonder.

Prior to the school camp, Ayanokouji hadn't even been on Hashimoto's radar. He'd barely known what he looked like. He remembered that Ayanokouji ran a fierce race against the former student council president during the sports festival, but that was it, and Hashimoto wasn't about to drastically change his evaluation of someone just because they were a fast runner. More importantly, he didn't pay Ayanokouji much mind because both Sakayanagi and Ryuuen, who had keen instincts when it came to sussing out other powerful people, didn't seem to be paying Ayanokouji any extra attention.

However, something had happened recently to make him change his mind about Ayanokouji. A puzzling remark made by the student council president, Nagumo Miyabi. Miyabi had made a mysterious claim that Horikita Manabu held Ayanokouji in higher regard than he did anyone else. Hashimoto tried to dismiss the idea as nothing more than a joke, but he couldn't do it.

In retrospect, the signs were all there. Why did Ayanokouji and the former student council president directly confront one another during the sports festival relay? What if that wasn't mere coincidence, but intentional? What if there was a reason they'd wanted to make a big show of competing against one another? Those questions began to swirl around in Hashimoto's head.

Additionally, he remained unsure about the matter of Ishizaki and the others supposedly overthrowing Ryuuen. Class C had been Class D, the lowest-ranked class by far, back in the spring. But they began steadily closing the gap between them and the upper-level classes. What if Ayanokouji had something to do with it...?

"What if he surpasses both Sakayanagi and Ryuuen...?" wondered Hashimoto.

As of this moment, he couldn't really imagine that happening. All he had to go on was mere suspicions; a series of paranoid delusions that might have gone too far. He was missing a crucial part of the puzzle. Nagumo's words might have been nothing more than an unfounded joke; what happened at the sports festival relay might just have been a product of Hashimoto's imagination.

Which was why he was taking action to discover the truth.

While acting under Sakayanagi's orders to spread rumors about Ichinose, Hashimoto had recently found himself with some free time to spare. He'd spent it following Ayanokouji around to try to find out what he was up to. Now, he arrived at Class C, only to find Ayanokouji was already gone.

"You never waste any time, huh, Ayanokouji?"

Perhaps because his circle of friends was rather limited, Ayanokouji hardly ever stayed back in the classroom after classes ended for the day. Was he with that close group of friends of his again today, Hashimoto wondered, the one including Miyake and Yukimura and the others? But Yukimura and Sakura were still in the classroom, so he eliminated that possibility.

"Yo, Hirata." Just standing there idly and observing another class would draw attention to himself, so Hashimoto quickly called out to Hirata, who hadn't yet left to go to his club.

"Oh, hey there, Hashimoto-kun. What's up?" replied Hirata.

"Just came by to check and see whether you got yourself a new girlfriend."

"Well, I'm not really thinking about jumping into another relationship right now."

"So you're still in the process of mending your broken heart, eh?"

"Ha ha... Something like that, I suppose," said Hirata.

"You'll have to tell me more about it sometime, then. Oh, by the way, I've been trying to get contact info for the guys I was with back at the school camp. I was thinking I'd ask Ayanokouji next, but it looks like he's already left," said Hashimoto.

"You didn't bump into him? I think he only just left a minute or two ago..."

Just a hair too late, then. Hashimoto, quickly determining that he might still be able to catch up to Ayanokouji, thanked Hirata and immediately stepped back out into the hallway.

It was almost time for the year-end exams. Even he

couldn't afford to spend every day doing nothing but chasing after Ayanokouji. He wanted to come to a definite conclusion, and he wanted to do so quickly, so he could shift his attention to prepping for the exams and be ready to take them in top form.

"Man, hope I get something soon," he muttered to himself.

If there was a chance, he would take it. And so he continued chasing after Ayanokouji.

As luck would have it, Ayanokouji was by the entrance, fiddling with his phone. Was he waiting to meet with someone? Or was he just killing time? Either way, it seemed like Hashimoto's luck was holding.

Ayanokouji was almost incessantly fiddling with his phone to communicate with people. It was unclear whether he was talking to Miyake and the other people in that group, or if he was communicating with someone who Hashimoto didn't know. The only thing he did know for sure was that Ayanokouji was an extremely easy person for him to track.

He'd been tailing several students so far: Katsuragi, Ryuuen, Kanzaki, and sometimes even Ichinose. None of them were all that easy to follow. If he got a bead on them once in two days, he considered himself lucky. And sometimes, when they gave him the slip, he'd go almost a whole week without knowing what they were up to.

However, Ayanokouji's daily routine was ironclad, and his circle of friends was extremely small. This made it incredibly easy to anticipate where he was going to be. On top of that, Ayanokouji seemed to have no awareness whatsoever of what was going on around him. He never paid attention to anything behind him, and he never gave any indication of having a keen sense of intuition, not even that he had *accidentally* detected Hashimoto following him.

Even so, Hashimoto wasn't so careless as to let his guard down. He followed Ayanokouji while keeping sufficient distance between them, just to be completely safe.

Then, his phone rang. It was one of his classmates, Shimizu Naoki.

"Hey, what's up, Naoki?"

"Well... To tell you the truth, it's about what happened this morning... Seriously, dude, I give up. This sucks."

"I know, dude. Hey, it's probably best just to forget about it, all right? We just have a lot of people who like to talk in our class is all."

A minor problem had cropped up that morning in Class A, which Hashimoto belonged to. Apparently, the girls of Class A had found out that Shimizu had confessed his feelings to one of their classmates, a girl named

Nishikawa. And that she'd turned him down. Nishikawa had probably inadvertently let the fact of Shimizu's confession slip out to her friends, and it had spread. It happened all the time.

"Dude, you're never going to get anyone to go out with you if you worry about each and every little thing, you know?" said Hashimoto.

"Y-yeah, I guess so, but... Seriously dude, I just can't forgive Nishikawa for this."

"Well, as much as I'd love to stick around and listen to you complain, I'm kind of in the middle of something right now."

"Oh, really? Sorry, man."

Hashimoto promised that he'd call him back that night and then ended the call.

"That's just what happens when you ask someone out without first making sure you've met all the conditions for success," he muttered after he hung up.

Resolving to console Shimizu later, Hashimoto followed Ayanokouji back to the dormitory.

"If he's heading straight back, then I guess I'm not getting anything today either, huh?"

The worst part of tailing Ayanokouji was probably the almost complete lack of variety. However, the elevator had passed the fourth floor, the location of Ayanokouji's room. It continued to ascend for a while. Hashimoto watched the monitor, observing Ayanokouji getting off alone on a floor where the girls were residing.

"If I remember correctly... That's Ichinose's floor, isn't it?" he said aloud.

It might be a coincidence. Ayanokouji might be meeting some other girl. But given what had been happening lately, Hashimoto couldn't help but connect the dots to Ichinose, even if he didn't want to.

"Since it's Ichinose, though, I guess it's possible he's just paying a simple visit...?"

While Ayanokouji had a small circle of friends, Ichinose was highly popular, liked by students across all grade levels. It wouldn't be surprising for her to be friends with Ayanokouji. Also, she was pretty cute. Plenty of students might be making a point of visiting her, maybe hoping to spark something by doing so.

Regardless, Ayanokouji got back on the elevator soon after. This time, he got off at the fourth floor, which was where his room was.

"What...?"

Hashimoto struggled to understand what in the world Ayanokouji was doing. On the monitor, he saw several girls from Class B entering the elevator from the floor Ichinose resided on. Hashimoto deduced that they'd come to visit her before Ayanokouji, causing him to decide to turn back when he bumped into them.

Just in case, Hashimoto quickly took the elevator up to the fourth floor. But Ayanokouji was gone, almost certainly back in his room.

"In the end, I got nothing today either, huh," he muttered.

After pondering whether or not to call it quits for now, he decided to mull over the situation for a while in the lobby. It was still early. There was still a good chance that Ayanokouji would make contact with Ichinose later, or that he might be making plans to go out and see someone else. If Ayanokouji hopped on the elevator, Hashimoto would be able to see whether he was headed up or down on the monitor.

His decision to hang around a bit longer paid off just about an hour later. Ayanokouji got on the elevator and began descending toward a lower floor. Additionally, he was still in his uniform.

"Is he heading back to the school building?"

It made no sense for him to be heading back out now, after going through all the trouble of heading back to the dorms. If he were headed to the convenience store and didn't want to bother changing his clothes, that might explain it...but Ayanokouji had his school bag with him.

Hashimoto immediately got up off the sofa and hid near the emergency stairs.

"All right, here's hoping something interesting is about to happen," he said.

As if Hashimoto's wish had just been granted, Ayanokouji exited the lobby and walked toward a relatively isolated area of campus. This pretty much put paid to the possibility of him heading to the school building or the convenience store. So was he meeting with someone? But...the place he was headed really wasn't well suited to casual hangouts.

All things considered, Hashimoto was sure he was up to something, and that he was meeting someone. If it turned out to be the former student council president Horikita, or Ryuuen, then things would be heating up for sure.

His expectations, however, were overturned quite unexpectedly.

"Whoa, whoa, are you serious...?" he murmured aloud.

The person who turned up to meet Ayanokouji was none other than Karuizawa Kei, from first-year Class C. She was quite the hot topic, even in Class A, after recently breaking up with Hirata. Hashimoto had had almost no contact with her himself, so he couldn't control his surprise at her unexpected appearance.

Disappointment washed over him. His expectations had been totally shattered.

This had nothing to do with the "hidden side" of Ayanokouji that he'd been trying to discover. This was simply a romantic affair. Hashimoto tried automatically to arrive at a different interpretation for the scene before him, but no matter how he looked at it, he couldn't help but feel like the two of them shared something more than a regular friendship. He'd witnessed Hirata and Karuizawa on dates several times before, but never sensed much intimacy between them or gotten the feeling they were lovers.

"...I don't get it. Why Ayanokouji?"

Which of them was romantically interested in the other? Or were they both interested in each other? Hashimoto tried to hazard a guess, but came up blank. Romance was never logical, anyway. After all, if he were to objectively compare Hirata and Ayanokouji, 80 percent of girls would probably choose Hirata. The remaining 20 percent might choose Ayanokouji as an alternative to having nothing at all. In short...

"The person who Ayanokouji has been in frequent contact with is Karuizawa...?"

Hashimoto quickly ditched that idea. It was just his imagination. Just something he had selfishly latched onto to explain the current situation. He needed to investigate further to know the truth.

However, he couldn't hear the details of their conversation. It wasn't like he could just casually stroll up close to them either, since this was a place students didn't often frequent.

"What should I do...?" he mused aloud. No matter how hard he tried, he was at a loss.

Then the scene took an unexpected turn.

"Chocolates, huh?" said Hashimoto.

Karuizawa handed Ayanokouji something she had been holding. Today was February 14th. If she was handing him something in secret, where no one was around to see, then he could easily guess what it was even without seeing what it was inside. If nothing else, this proved that Karuizawa had developed a romantic interest in Ayanokouji.

"Well, guess that's it for today, then."

It was completely unrelated to the information that Hashimoto had sought to discover. But just as he came to that conclusion and thought to head on back to the dorm, he stopped in his tracks.

"Since I've got this chance...maybe I should try to pick a fight with him?"

Considering how close they were to the year-end exams, it could be said that this was a valuable opportunity.

He could shake things up, throw Ayanokouji off balance by forcibly dragging Karuizawa into the equation. This was a chance to expose Ayanokouji's secrets. And if nothing came of it...then he might be able to conclude once and for all that Ayanokouji was no threat to him.

His mind made up, Hashimoto quickly headed over toward Ayanokouji and Karuizawa.

7.1

I SENSED SOMEONE APPROACHING US from behind, moving quickly. It was obvious from their movement that they didn't want to miss the chance to see me and Kei in close proximity to each other like this.

"Yo, Karuizawa. Oh, and Ayanokouji too."

It was Hashimoto, who had been hiding his presence and tailing after me since I left the lobby.

"...Uh, who is he?" Kei, not seeming to know who Hashimoto was, looked to me for an answer.

"Hashimoto, from Class A. I was with him during the school camp."

After greeting us, Hashimoto approached Kei.

"Whoa, for a guy and a girl to have a secret rendezvous like this... you're quite the smooth operator, aren't ya, Ayanokouji?"

I'd known Hashimoto would try to make contact eventually. So this was the moment he'd chosen, huh? In that case, I'd just have to turn his plans to my own benefit.

"It's not like we're really doing any—"

"Don't try to hide it. It's Valentine's Day. Even if you're not dating, I'm not surprised you two set up a whole secret rendezvous. In fact, it looks like you got something from her," said Hashimoto. He'd witnessed me receiving chocolate from Kei and immediately putting it in my bag.

"She just happened to give me chocolates by coincidence. It wasn't like we were meeting intentionally."

I tried to deny it, but Hashimoto snickered, seeing through my excuse. "No, come on, man. You *knew* she was going to be giving you chocolates from the very beginning, didn't you? I mean, your bag."

"My bag?"

"You already went back to your dorm room, so there was no reason for you to bring your school bag when you went back out. Right?"

"...Well, I was actually planning on heading over to the library originally. It's just that Karuizawa called me right before I left, and I agreed to meet her. That's what happened."

"So...you're saying it's just a coincidence, then?"

I nodded in response to Hashimoto's question, then took two books out of my school bag, showing them to him.

"Well, it's all the same, in any case. You still got chocolate from Karuizawa, anyway." From Hashimoto's point of view, it didn't matter that I hadn't been the one who reached out to Karuizawa. What mattered was the fact that I had gotten chocolate from her.

"I don't really get it, but... Is there some kind of problem?" I asked.

"I'm just curious about why she's attracted to you is all. I mean, come on, Karuizawa's ex is Hirata. One of the most popular guys in the entire school, you know? So, what, she picks you after dumping Hirata?"

So he wanted to know how things had gotten to this point. Kei, who had been listening in silence so far, opened her mouth to speak.

"Uh, sorry, but I think there's kind of a misunderstanding here."

"Misunderstanding?"

"Yeah. I actually meant to give the chocolate to Hirata-kun originally. But I kinda thought it would be, like, a waste to just throw it away. So, I thought I'd give it to someone, and I just happened to choose Ayanokouji-kun," said Kei.

"You hand over an intimate gift like chocolate, and then say it was just at random? And in a place like this, on top of that? Come on, that's a lie. And it's a pretty lame one too," said Hashimoto with a laugh.

Kei looked visibly angry.

"Excuse me?" she demanded, pinning him with an intense look. "Where do you get off, just showing up out of nowhere and spouting nonsense at us? What in the hell is your deal?"

"I just want to know the truth," said Hashimoto, looking a little cowed.

All things said and done, it was true that we'd done nothing to hide the suspicious circumstances of our meeting. I pivoted and came at things from another direction. This would be a chance for Kei to prove her skills. Prove how well she could keep up with me.

"Come on. Don't you think it's best if you're honest about what's going on here, Karuizawa? I think it'll just come back to bite us later if we try to hide it?" I told Kei, handing the baton to her. "I mean, if *he* thinks we're dating, then that'll be bad, right?"

Without hesitation, she let out a dramatic sigh.

"Agh. All right, all right. I'll come out with it. But this does *not* get spread around, okay?" said Kei, pointing her finger at Hashimoto. "I'm entrusting the chocolate to

Ayanokouji-kun to hold on to. So that he can give it to the person I like."

"So... you're saying that Ayanokouji is the middleman?" he asked.

"Yes, exactly. Get the picture?" said Kei.

The look on Hashimoto's face seemed to say that he just couldn't believe it.

"Okay, then, who's the chocolate actually for?" he said, continuing to press us.

"Huh? I'm not going to tell that to someone I just met. Are you an idiot or something?" said Kei. She was clearly trying to agitate him, but nothing about her response rang false. It was all in accordance with the image of the popular *gyaru* that Karuizawa Kei had constructed for herself.

"That's... Well, I suppose you've got a point," said Hashimoto, looking somewhat shocked. He bowed his head apologetically.

"Okay, look, you're not gonna smooth this all over just by bowing your head at me. Seriously, give me a break," said Kei.

"...I see. It seems like I really misunderstood things here. Sorry 'bout that. When I thought that you two might like each other, I just couldn't help but get suspicious," said Hashimoto.

"Okay, and why are you sticking your nose in something that has nothing to do with you in the first place?" said Kei.

"Well, regarding that point, you can't really say that it's got nothing to do with me."

"Huh?"

Hashimoto walked toward the still-angry Kei. He reached out his arm and pushed against the wall, blocking Kei in.

"Hey, wh-what? What is it?"

"You know, I've been thinking about this for a while now. Go out with me, Karuizawa. I don't know who your next true love might be, but if you haven't given anyone your chocolate yet, then that means you haven't expressed your feelings. Isn't that right?" He kept going, adding forcefully, "It's not too late, even now."

"What are you even talking about...? You seriously think I'd be okay with that?!"

"Love's an interesting thing, because you never know what's going to happen. You know?" said Hashimoto, shooting a sharp glance at me for an instant. He might be trying to provoke a response from me by aggressively hitting on Kei.

"Well, I'll be going then," I said.

"Huh? W-wait, I'm heading back too."

Kei put her hand to Hashimoto's chest, forcibly pushed him back, and then took her distance from him.

"That was cold," said Hashimoto, with a bitter smile on his face. It didn't seem like he intended to keep pushing things any further today. Or rather, it seemed like he no longer had any interest in Kei.

Kei surveyed the situation, deliberately let out an exasperated sigh, and then headed on back to the dorms.

"Sorry," Hashimoto said to me. "For butting in and all, at such a bad time."

"Nah, no big deal."

We walked side by side until the point where the path to the dormitory and the school building split.

"Anyway, seems like you've got a lot to worry about in your love life too, huh?" asked Hashimoto.

"What are you saying?"

He put his hand on my shoulder, and whispered in my ear, "I'm talking 'bout how an inexperienced girl probably won't be able to take your huge you-know-what, dude." He wore a smile on his face, as if he were teasing me.

Seriously, this again...?

"Hey, dude, don't look so exasperated about it. You know, there's quite a few people tipping their hat to you because of it," he added.

That didn't make me at all happy to know. If anything, I was starting to resent the school camp more and more for causing this to happen.

"So, anyway, King. Exchange contact info with me," said Hashimoto.

"I'll do it as long as you never use that nickname you just suddenly came up with ever again," I replied.

"Ha ha ha ha! All right, I won't, I won't."

I went ahead and swapped contact information with Hashimoto, who apologized to me as he pulled out his cell phone.

"Welp, guess I'll be heading on back then. See ya later, Ayanokouji," he said and left.

Hashimoto came and went, like a passing storm. Did he think he'd collected enough information for now? Or did he just want to avoid pushing the issue any further?

Regardless, my true nature should remain shrouded in mystery in his mind for now. As long as things continued this way, of course.

I decided to stop by the library and see Hiyori, who was probably there waiting for me. There was also one other person whom I had promised to meet at school.

7.2

∙ ∙

SINCE I'D GOTTEN BACK to the dorms later than planned, I couldn't meet up with the Ayanokouji Group after all. When I made it back to my room just before seven o'clock, I saw a paper bag had been placed in front of my door. Within it were two differently wrapped packages, one square and one round.

Each package had names handwritten on them. They were Valentine's chocolates from Haruka and Airi, as I'd already been alerted to by messages posted in our chat. Akito and Keisei had received the same thing.

I entered my room and lined up the chocolates on top of my desk.

"I never expected to get five..." I said aloud.

Kei, Airi, Haruka, Hiyori. And one more. It was a box of chocolates that was wrapped with a lovely pink ribbon.

Later that night, after ten o'clock, I stepped out into the hallway with a hoodie on over my casual clothes. I got in the elevator, knowing the cameras inside it were placed in such a way that my face was hidden. Just a precautionary measure in the unlikely event that something did happen. I would have preferred to have this meeting elsewhere, but if she was resting because she didn't feel well, then it couldn't be helped.

It was late enough that Ichinose might already be asleep, but I'd confirmed that she was still awake ahead of time by sending her a message, having gotten her contact information from Horikita. However, I didn't tell her that I was coming to her room.

I got to Ichinose's floor and stood in front of her door.

I rang the doorbell. Ten seconds passed. Then twenty seconds. I heard nothing from inside the room, so I rang the doorbell once again. I supposed it was only natural that Ichinose might be confused about someone coming to visit her in the middle of the night.

After about thirty seconds had passed, I decided to speak up.

"Hey, it's me, Ichinose. It's Ayanokouji."

It was past curfew. Hanging out on her floor for too long could get me in trouble, and Ichinose probably understood that. She wouldn't carelessly abandon someone to face that kind of danger.

"...Ayanokouji... kun? What's up?" replied Ichinose, her voice coming from the other side of the door.

She sounded weak, and I heard her begin to cough immediately after. It was hard to tell just from how she sounded if she was really ill, though.

"There are a few important things I'd like to talk to you about. I was hoping I could come in and talk to you. Is that not okay?"

"No, it's fine... um..."

"To tell the truth, it'll be bad if another girl sees me out here," I said, urging her more forcefully.

"Wait just a second, okay?"

Moments later, I heard the sound of the lock being disengaged from inside the room. When Ichinose opened the door, she looked so visibly down in the dumps that I almost couldn't believe it.

"Nyahaha. You were being a little aggressive there, Ayanokouji-kun..." she mumbled. She was wearing a surgical mask, clearly not feeling well. Seemed like she wasn't faking being sick after all.

"Sorry about that. I was definitely a bit aggressive. You really don't look like you're feeling that well, huh," I told her.

"Yeah... I'm just a little bit of a mess right now..."

"Sorry for visiting you at such a bad time."

"No, no, it's okay. My fever has mostly subsided. I guess it's more like I just feel all bleh because I slept way too much, and I'm hungry? Oh, I'm sorry to ask this, but could you put this mask on?" said Ichinose.

She presented me with a mask, so that I wouldn't catch her cold. My immune system was pretty robust, but I wasn't immune to illness, and I was sure Ichinose would feel awful if I thoughtlessly refused her request and then did catch her cold. I put the mask on without a moment's hesitation.

"So have you been to the clinic?"

"I went there during the week."

A lot of students thought that Ichinose was faking being sick to get away from all the rumors circulating about her. Apparently, that wasn't the case. She was genuinely sick.

"You were worried that I've been missing class because of those rumors, huh? Thanks for worrying about me," said Ichinose.

"No, I..."

Did she see through me and guess what I was thinking?

"You're the first person who I've met with face-to-face like this since I've been sick, Ayanokouji-kun," she said.

"Is that so?"

"There were some girls who came back to visit me when my fever was pretty bad, but even though I felt bad about it, I had to turn them away since I wasn't feeling up to it. Since then, I guess my other friends must think I'm feeling depressed, because it seems like they've been holding back from coming by," said Ichinose.

I'd come to visit her much later than everyone else, and yet, I was her first visitor since she'd gotten sick, huh? Ironic.

The situation seemed simple enough: Ichinose was resting because she was sick. But when I considered her past behavior, I didn't have to think too hard to come to the realization that she was the kind of person who paid careful consideration to monitoring her health. Not to mention that the year-end exams were right around the corner. She would have wanted to avoid getting sick at all costs during a time like this, leaving me certain that she'd caught a cold because her immune system had been weakened by the psychological ordeal she was suffering.

Not that she was going to admit that, of course. "I'm not going to take a day off just because of those rumors," said Ichinose.

"You're really tough," I told her.

"Tough, huh...? Oh, sorry, but could you please close the entranceway door for me? I had it open to ventilate the room a bit, but now it's gotten a bit cold... Oh, and please make sure you wash your hands thoroughly after you get back," she replied.

"Okay."

She had been running the humidifier inside the room to prevent it from getting too dry. The flu virus thrives best in dry, low-temperature environments, and warming the air around you is, therefore, an excellent way to eliminate that virus. If you scoffed at the idea of taking such precautions, then you dramatically increased your chances of prolonging your cold or passing it to someone who came to visit. The dryness of the air was the main reason why colds tended to last longer in the winter.

That said, it was a little odd that I'd been visiting girls' rooms *and* having girls come to my room so often of late, and yet absolutely none of those visits had had anything to do with romance.

"Is something wrong...?" asked Ichinose, giving me a puzzled look as I examined her humidifier.

"I'm sorry that I came by and bothered you while you're resting," I replied.

"Oh, no, it's okay, really. It's true that it would be safer if I didn't meet with anyone right now, but it's probably a better idea for me to actually let people know I caught a cold, I suppose."

It seemed she was well aware of the widespread speculation that she was faking being sick. As if to prove it, Ichinose showed me her phone. It looked like she'd had several exchanges with Horikita. I guessed that Horikita was still worried about Ichinose and was showing it in her own way.

We didn't talk for long after that. I decided to leave as soon as possible and did so at the next good opportunity that presented itself.

THE DAY OF THE PRACTICE test had come—a day on which each class would have to focus on their own exam. However, the classroom was full of students engaged in chattering, rather than studying. And they weren't talking about things like vocabulary and test preparation either. The topics of conversation I overheard were all completely unrelated to the exams.

"It's pretty lively in here, huh," I said aloud.

"Well, of course it is," said Horikita. "Isn't it obvious? It's because of the crazy rumors we've been hearing this morning."

"Crazy rumors? More news about Ichinose?"

"No. New rumors, and they're causing chaos within Class C."

"New rumors...huh." Just a glance at the total chaos

that was our classroom made it clear this was no small thing.

"By the way, it seems they mention you, Ayanokouji-kun," said Horikita, showing me her phone. There were four rumors described on her notes app.

"This is—"

Ayanokouji Kiyotaka has a crush on Karuizawa Kei.

Hondou Ryoutarou is only interested in chubby girls.

Shinohara Satsuki engaged in prostitution when she was in junior high.

Satou Maya hates Onodera Kayano.

The contents of the rumors were similar in nature. Four people, including me, were singled out and named directly as objects of ridicule.

"Where did this information come from?" I asked.

"Do you know about the bulletin boards that the school provides for each of the classes?"

"Yeah, if I recall, they're in the app, right?"

When students wanted to check the balance remaining on their account, or something of the sort, they had to log in through the official school app. This app included forums and bulletin boards for student use, but because we had plenty of easy-to-use chat apps on our phones, the bulletin boards went ignored 99 percent of the time.

"That was a good catch, noticing those posts. Who was the first person to discover them?"

"By the time I got to the classroom, the rumors were already doing the rounds. I wonder if someone just happened to stumble upon the messages on the bulletin board when they were using the app? Also, you can tell when the board was last updated, apparently."

The bulletin boards weren't just used for classwork—there were several dedicated just to casual chatter. Since anyone could access them, there was a good chance these rumors had been seen by the other classes too.

"Aren't you curious about why the modus operandi this time around is different from the last time?"

"Regardless of whether this was committed by the same person or by someone else, there are countless ways to spread rumors. Sure, the modus operandi's different, but there's nothing we can really do about that, right? Additionally, since these rumors were put in explicit words and posted online, they're impossible to conceal or dismiss."

Horikita pivoted, prefacing her next comment with a disclaimer. "By the way. I'm asking you this just in case, but is it true?"

"No, it's not." I denied it right away. "Besides, not many

people even know Karuizawa and I are on speaking terms to begin with."

"Can you think of anyone who might have posted those rumors?"

"Well, I suppose I have some guesses."

I gave Horikita a brief summary of what happened yesterday when I met up with Hashimoto.

"If Hashimoto-kun started the rumors about Ichinose-san, then it wouldn't be surprising at all for him to do the same with rumors about you and Karuizawa-san."

"But what about the other victims? We don't have a lot of avenues to ascertain the truth."

"That's true..."

I mean, it wasn't like there were any students who could just directly confirm the truth of these rum—

"Hey, Shinohara! You used to be a prostitute or something?!" shouted Yamauchi with a laugh, completely oblivious to other people's feelings, as usual.

"I-I was *not*!" replied Shinohara, fervently denying it. She stood from her seat in a panic, embarrassment and anger writ large on her face.

"Well, show me some proof then," said Yamauchi.

"Proof...? How am I supposed to prove it to you?!" shouted Shinohara.

Captivated by the drama, the students already in the classroom started sharing the rumors with the ones who were just showing up. Well, they'd hear them sooner or later, anyway.

"So you're saying it's all a lie?" Yamauchi demanded. "Then what, everything else posted online was a lie too, huh? And that we're just running our mouths without even thinking?"

As I watched Yamauchi and Shinohara get into it, I confirmed what I was thinking with Horikita.

"I wonder... Well, I suppose all we can do is confirm the truth of the rumors with each student in turn, like what Yamauchi is doing."

Of course, it was easier said than done for a normal person to go around prying into people's private business, reopening wounds they wanted to keep hidden for all to see.

"How stupid can you be?! I can't believe you're getting carried away by these rumors when you don't even know who wrote them!"

Shinohara was clearly furious with Yamauchi, but it wasn't surprising she was denying it so vehemently. If anything, it was surprising that she could be this calm after someone had posted such things about her.

"But you know...don't you think all the stuff said online is pretty believable?"

"Knock it off already, Haruki!"

In response to Yamauchi's merciless teasing, Ike, who had been standing next to him, aggressively grabbed him by the shoulders and tried to get him to stop.

"Wh-what, dude?! This is just my chance to pay Shinohara back for always acting so high and mighty all the time!"

"Payback for what...? Dude, those rumors are nothing but lies!"

"And how do you know that, huh? I mean, they do say ugly chicks like her can get up to some surprisingly nasty shit, y'know." Yamauchi laughed, continuing to run his mouth like a fool in complete dismissal of Ike's feelings. "Oh, ho, I get it. Ike, you kinda have a thing for Shinohara. That's why you can't admi—"

"Haruki!" Ike grabbed Yamauchi's collar.

"Knock it off, you two!"

Unable to stand by and watch things play out, Sudou stepped in and pulled the two of them apart by force.

Hirata arrived at the classroom soon after and immediately sensed what was going on. He began asking some of the girls about the situation, confirming the specifics of these rumors.

Since Shinohara was denying everything, Yamauchi temporarily switched targets. "So, hey, Hondou! You seriously have a fat fetish?" he said, directing his attention toward Hondou.

"N-no way, dude! No way! Those rumors are all just straight-up BS! Right, Ayanokouji? I mean, there's no way that you have a thing for Karuizawa!"

Naturally, Hondou denied the accusation. He also turned to me for help, seeking to avoid persecution. All at once, everyone's eyes were on me. Fortunately, most of Kei's group of friends still hadn't gotten to class yet.

I answered Hondou with a nod, confirming that he was right. He shouted "See?" loudly, turning back to Yamauchi.

"Tch, come on. What the hell, man? Are they all lies?"

Now that three of us had denied the rumors, the classroom began to settle down a little.

"But...it's true that Satou-san doesn't really like Onodera-san very much, isn't it?" Maezono blurted out without thinking, probably because Onodera wasn't here yet.

"H-hey, wait a second, Maezono-san!" Satou frantically tried to stop her, but it was already too late.

"Actually yeah, come to think of it, has anyone ever seen Satou hang out with Onodera before?"

"Th-that's..."

The situation had changed. All of a sudden, people no longer seemed inclined to dismiss the rumors as outright lies. Sudou, confirming that he had separated Ike and Yamauchi, walked up to Horikita and me.

"Ayanokouji. You really don't have a thing for Karui-zawa?" Apparently, even he felt like he needed to ask.

"Nope, I don't."

"Hm. Well, hey, even if it was true, it doesn't really matter to me, I guess. Hey, Suzune."

"What is it, Sudou-kun?"

"Well, it's just that I happened to hear a little bit of your conversation earlier. If you're okay with me helping out, I'd like to lend a hand," said Sudou.

"Meaning?"

"Well, I'm an insensitive guy. So I can just go around and ask people straight out, like Haruki did. How about it?" offered Sudou.

It was true that Sudou could be a useful tool in determining the origin of these rumors...though if he had heard our conversation, he should have heard the part where I denied the fact that I was interested in Kei.

"Don't do anything to lower yourself in people's estimation," Horikita said. "People already don't think too highly of you. You should be striving to improve how they see you, even if just a little. Yamauchi-kun's careless comments seem to have drastically lowered his standing in our class..."

It felt like Yamauchi had overtaken Sudou as the most hated person in class in one fell swoop. Even Ike, his closest friend, was now furious at him.

"You might be right about that... But I want to be useful somehow."

Sudou glanced at me for a moment before immediately averting his gaze. I was sure it was because he was vaguely aware of the fact that Horikita consulted me on a lot of things. Of course, he probably also understood that it was partly because it was easy for us to talk to one another, being desk neighbors.

"In that case, please keep an eye on Yamauchi-kun and keep him under control. If even one of the rumors had been positive, this would be a different story. Instead, they're so troubling as to become deeply personal, whether or not they're true. I'm sure Hondou-kun must be shaken by all this, so I'd like you to check in on him. You can do that, right?"

"...Yeah, okay."

Sudou seemed a little bit disappointed, but he still obediently followed Horikita's instructions. Horikita waited to confirm that he'd left, then returned to the topic at hand.

"This is likely part of Sakayanagi-san's plan. She wasn't satisfied with going after Ichinose-san, so she's trying the same scheme on Class C too. Hitting multiple people at the same time, no less. I think it's just an attempt to throw us off before the year-end exams, but... What should we do?"

"What do you mean? Do you think there's any way we can really fight these rumors? The more we try to deny them, the more everyone's imaginations will run wild, convincing them they're true. The rumor about mc isn't really a big deal, but if the ones about the other students are recognized as fact, it'll do them some real damage."

"...That's true. You might be right." Horikita nodded in understanding as she looked over at Hondou and Shinohara. I wonder if she was imagining herself in their shoes. "That said, this is a really dirty move. How do we push back against something like this?"

"I wonder."

"Even though you can see the sparks starting to fly, you're planning to just sit back and watch?" asked Horikita.

"It's not that bad. Well, I guess it will be from Karuizawa's point of view, though."

"Meaning you're fine?"

"Yep, totally fine."

For whatever reason, it seemed like Horikita might have been hoping to see me panic. As a result, I got to see a rare look of mild disappointment on her face.

"It's fortunate that it's not the other way around, at least," she said.

In other words, if the rumor had claimed Kei had a crush on me. That would've inspired more rumors about Kei—that she was chasing after a new guy right after breaking up with Hirata, for instance. Speculation would run rampant. It didn't matter if something was completely untrue; if enough people recognized a lie as fact, that lie would become reality.

"But...I can't just sit back in silence and observe forever, like you."

"I see."

The commotion in the classroom made it obvious these fires were going to keep spreading even if no one took action. Yamauchi was about to turn the conversation back toward Shinohara and Satou, but Hirata stopped him.

"Yamauchi-kun. Just because something is written on the bulletin board doesn't make it true. Besides, at the very least, you can agree that it's wrong to hurt a fellow classmate like this, right?" said Hirata.

"But if it's like with the rumors about Ichinose, then everyone's gotta have heard them already, right? Even if we don't say anything, it'll all be the same in the end, won't it?"

"I don't think we can say that for sure. At least not yet. That's why I think the best thing for us to do right now is to carry on without letting what was posted on the bulletin board throw us into chaos," said Hirata.

His words were met with a strong chorus of agreement from both the guys and girls. This wasn't going to solve all of our problems, of course, but he'd at least managed to put a lid on things for now.

Then Horikita got a message on her phone.

"It's from Kanzaki-kun." Horikita took a look at the message. "Apparently, it seems like Ichinose has taken today off as well."

The day of the practice test. Even if you were feeling a little under the weather, you would still want to take the test to check where your abilities were at. Not to mention the fact that Ichinose was the class leader, the one responsible for guiding her classmates along. Well, based on how she looked yesterday, it was no wonder she hadn't completely recovered yet.

"And one more thing... It seems like similar rumors were posted on the Class B bulletin board."

"Meaning they must've noticed what was written about us too."

"Seems that way."

Horikita hurriedly logged into the app and checked the Class B bulletin board. Much like with Class C, there were four rumors posted on the boards, each naming a different student. There were similar messages on Class D's bulletin board, too.

"Conveniently enough, it looks like the students of Class A were the only ones who had no rumors posted about them. Can I have a moment of your time after class today? I'd like to check in with Ichinose, get some more information, and discuss how to respond to these posts."

"Sure," I agreed.

"For the time being, let's focus on the practice test. It's a valuable opportunity to gauge the difficulty level of the year-end exam, and to get an idea of where our class is at."

But Horikita wasn't one of the people targeted by the rumors. Unlike her, the victims weren't going to be able to concentrate on the test quite so easily. When Kei and her friends arrived at the classroom, they huddled together and started whispering among themselves. Then, they looked over at me. They looked at me as if I were human trash. I could tell what was going on even if I couldn't hear what they were saying.

"Does it really look like Ayanokouji-kun has a crush on Karuizawa-san?"

"Hey, what do you think about him anyway? Huh, Karuizawa-san?"

I was sure the conversation they were having right now went something like that. And, without a doubt, I bet that Kei was responding to them with things like "He's disgusting" or "He's the worst."

"Didn't you say that you were fine?"

"...It kinda bothers me a little."

I would've kept watching them talking, but I didn't want to actually overhear what they were saying, so I decided to stop. The real issue was the students other than me who'd been singled out by name and were currently being discussed.

7.4

THE PRACTICE TEST had begun, despite the chilly traces of awkwardness and ill will still lingering in the air. This was an important phase of the end of the school year. The content of the practice test was, even comparatively speaking, much more difficult than what we'd seen on tests so far. Extremely so.

However, it was also true that students who'd gotten through the exams we've had so far should be able to handle what was on this one without needing to panic. On the other hand, the students who'd barely managed to squeak by probably needed to really put their noses to the grindstone after this practice test.

I'd been invited to join the Ayanokouji Group for a study session, but I decided to let them know they could start without me, since I was going to be accompanying

Horikita today. Kanzaki didn't want to draw any attention to himself, so we decided to meet up at the Keyaki Mall after school, after the practice tests were over.

Following Horikita's lead, we went over to where Kanzaki was waiting for us. He was by the southern entrance to the mall. This was the farthest point from the school building, so students didn't usually come by here.

I wasn't particularly invested in the whole class conflict thing, but that didn't mean that I wasn't worried about Ichinose, as a friend. Besides, more information wasn't a bad thing. Not to mention the fact that Hashimoto had been tailing me lately, and for some time now. If I made contact with Class B, the shadow of Class A would inevitably loom closer...but that was exactly what I was hoping for.

In fact, Hashimoto had followed me all the way here, keeping an appropriate level of distance all the while.

"Two days off in a row. And on top of that, you still haven't been able to get in touch with Ichinose-san yourself?"

"It's not that she isn't responding at all; it's that her responses are slow. All I've gotten from her was a notification that she's sick with a cold."

Kanzaki seemed on edge. I imagined he'd been under a lot of stress lately. Ichinose must have told him not to worry, but I supposed he could hardly sit there and take it.

Ichinose's health issues were probably one reason why she was reluctant to meet with any of her classmates right now. I was willing to bet another was that she really didn't want to hear about or discuss the rumors any further.

"What did your homeroom teacher say about it?"

"The same as always. She only said that Ichinose was taking the day off because she was out sick with a cold."

Their homeroom teacher had probably gotten the same message from Ichinose that everyone else had. Kanzaki looked depressed because he doubted whether Ichinose was really absent from class because she had a cold. After all, she'd been the subject of an ongoing scandal lately. Of course, he suspected that was the real reason for her absence.

"How about we go to visit her? I think we could clear this all up if we just went to see her in person," said Horikita.

"Apparently, some girls from our class went to visit her. It doesn't sound like they were able to see her face-to-face," replied Kanzaki.

Horikita, realizing that the situation wasn't looking good, pondered the matter deeply. "Well, on the bright side, Ichinose is academically gifted. Even if she doesn't take the practice test, she'll probably do just fine," she reasoned.

It was possible for students who were sick, like

Ichinose, to get the test questions at a later date, or they could ask other students about what problems were on the test.

"We're not worried about that either. We're only concerned about Ichinose's mental well-being," said Kanzaki.

As Horikita and Kanzaki continued to try to come up with a plan, several shadows approached us. It seemed like Hashimoto had already reported on this secret meeting.

"Oh, it sounds like Ichinose-san is absent from class again today, huh? Next week is the year-end exam. If she were absent for an extended period of time...why, perhaps all the way to the day of the exam... Well, she might be in a lot of trouble, hm?"

"...Sakayanagi."

Sakayanagi and her underlings had appeared before us. Well, before Kanzaki, rather. We saw Kamuro and Hashimoto with her, and also a boy named Kitou. So these were the key members of Sakayanagi's faction, huh?

"Now then, what in the world could you be discussing with these Class-C fellows?" asked Sakayanagi.

"It has nothing to do with you."

"Oh, my, it doesn't seem like we're very welcome here."

"If you want to be welcomed, then you should stop spreading weird rumors. Before you do something that you can't take back."

Sakayanagi and her classmates looked at one another and chuckled.

"What in the world are you talking about?" she asked.

"Class B's unity won't be shaken, no matter how many rumors you spread."

"I'm afraid I don't know what kind of situation your class is in. But I look forward to finding out what comes next."

I was guessing she'd only come here to see for herself how things were proceeding. She seemed to conclude that her plans were showing immediate results, for she departed right after that exchange with Kanzaki.

"Don't worry about her, Kanzaki-kun," said Horikita. "This is all part of Sakayanagi-san's strategy."

"I know."

Unfortunately, Kanzaki's concern for his companions, and his humble, reserved nature meant his suffering wouldn't be ending anytime soon.

CLASS WAS OVER, but it wasn't like the rumors were going to stop spreading. I made it back to the dorm and was relaxing when I got a call from Kei.

"Hey, w-w-w-wait a minute! What's going on, Kiyotaka?!"

"What do you mean, 'What's going on?'" I already knew, but I figured I'd anyway.

"No, come on, you know what! Kiyotaka, there's... well, um, there's a-a rumor going around that you have a c-crush on me! Did you not know?!"

"Don't worry about the rumors."

"N-no, no way, no way, no way! It's not like I can just *not* worry about it just because it's a rumor! How did this even happen?!"

She was shouting so loudly that there was a shrill

ringing in my ears. I moved my phone away for a moment and hit the button to lower the volume.

"I suppose it might be Hashimoto who started the rumor," I said. "Or maybe some other students saw us together."

"Aahhh!" Kei let out a quiet scream.

"Well, I mean, this is fine though, isn't it? It would've been really bad for you if things were reversed."

"R-reversed?"

"If the rumor went 'Kei has a crush on Kiyotaka,' then that'd be bad news for you, wouldn't it? I think if that were the case, then people would be even more suspicious of you than they are of me, since you just broke up with Hirata," I told her.

"...I-I suppose so, but..."

"Don't worry. Things like rumors always fade quickly."

"Really?"

"Still, I suppose it might be easier for us to make contact moving forward, thanks to this rumor. If I try to talk to you, people will just assume it's because of what the rumor says, and that'll be that."

It all came down to perspective. I had no plans to start having conversations in conspicuous locations, but it could be something of an insurance policy, circumstances depending.

"No, no, no, no, no, no, no!" Kei repeated the word many more times than before. "If the two of us are together, people will look at us weird! They absolutely, definitely will look at us weird!"

Was repeating yourself like that becoming some kind of trend? What a bizarre speech affectation. Anyway, this meant that Hashimoto, who'd been following me, would also have this information planted in his head.

"Don't worry about it."

"Even if you tell me not to worry about it........."

A long period of silence followed, after which she apparently decided it was just too difficult after all. "It's just impossible. I can't do it!"

Kei continued to grumble at me about a variety of topics for a while but then eventually seemed to give up, and she ended the call.

7.6

THINGS WERE BEGINNING to move at a dizzying pace. Even though there was no special exam, and we should be concentrating only on the written exam that was going to be held in late February, these were tumultuous days.

On Friday, February 18th—three days after the practice test—students from each class except for B had gathered at a spot some distance from the school building. Hirata had done his best to keep the new rumors from spreading at this critical juncture, but his efforts had been in vain. Class A, the only class with no rumors about them posted on the bulletin boards, had already gotten wind of the information.

"Yo, Ishizaki. So what the heck did you wanna talk about with me, anyway?" asked Hashimoto, seeming the same as always.

"What do I want to talk about? You already know what this is about, Hashimoto! And what are you thinkin', bringin' Kitou along with you? I told ya to come alone, didn't I?" said Ishizaki.

"Well, you brought Albert with you, didn't you? Just taking precautions."

The air was tense, like everyone was on tenterhooks. Looking at the current situation, it was hard to imagine the two of them had been rooming together just a little while ago at the school camp, but the reasons why things had gotten to be like this were plain to see.

"We just came to talk today. Isn't that right, Ishizaki-kun?"

Ishizaki and Albert weren't the only Class-D students present. Hiyori and Ibuki were there too.

"Well, as long as they don't make a scene, then I suppose everything will be fine."

"But..."

Hiyori's worries were understandable. Given the people who were present, it was hard to imagine *nothing* happening.

"But what about those other people? I didn't know you invited other people out here aside from us," said Ishizaki.

Hashimoto looked over at us and let out an exasperated sigh. "Dunno about them. Aren't you the ones who called them?"

Apparently, both Class D and Class A were uncomfortable about having us Class-C students present.

"It's just like you said, Ayanokouji," said Akito, who stood beside me, along with the rest of the Ayanokouji Group. We'd all met up at the café for a study session a little while ago.

"I just remembered that time when Kanzaki and Hashimoto were going at it. And then I just 'happened' to see you guys heading away from campus, so I thought that maybe... Well."

As soon as I'd told Akito that I had sensed something was wrong, he immediately followed me here. The only thing I hadn't planned on was Haruka, Airi, and Keisei coming along too.

"There's way more people here than there was last time. Things might get pretty rough..."

"Ah, come on, why do we keep getting into these kinds of dangerous situations all the time?" said Haruka, apparently exasperated.

"Well, whatever. It doesn't matter who called them here. So let's hear what you have to say, Shiina-chan."

"It's about the rumors. You Class-A people are the ones who've been starting them, aren't you?" said Hiyori, perhaps deciding this would result in a fistfight if she left it to Ishizaki to handle the conversation.

"Hey, hey, why are you asking us something like that?"

"That's friggin'—"

"Please leave this to me, Ishizaki-kun," said Hiyori, gently stopping Ishizaki from angrily shouting back. "I happened to overhear Kanzaki-kun saying that he saw you spreading rumors about Ichinose-san."

"Wow, he's a blabbermouth, huh? Or maybe you happened to hear that from those two over there?" replied Hashimoto. He was referring to me and Akito, since we'd heard Hashimoto's conversation with Kanzaki the other day.

"Please answer the question, Hashimoto-kun." Hiyori continued to press Hashimoto without even looking in our direction.

"...Well, Ayanokouji and Miyake know, so I'll just come out and say it, I suppose. I heard these rumors about Ichinose somewhere, and I just decided to repeat them a bunch, just 'cause I thought it'd be amusing."

Hashimoto didn't admit the truth, of course.

"That's a rather convenient excuse. Do you really think something like that is still going to fly?"

"Excuse? It's the truth. I guess if it's wrong to repeat rumors 'cause it amuses you, then I'm the bad guy. Still, it's strange, isn't it? That Class D, who should have nothing to do with this, would just swoop into this whole situation?" said Hashimoto. He continued talking, jovial as ever, but with a sharp glint in his eye. "Is it possible that...it's actually you Class-D folks who are the ones spreading those rumors?"

"You've got to be friggin' kidding me. We already know that Sakayanagi is the one spreading these rumors!"

"Don't be so quick to assume that. Sure, it's true that our leader is the aggressive type. There are times when she, against her better judgment, says things that'll provoke people. Says things against Ichinose too. I mean, I guess I understand how you feel. I understand why you wanna read way too much into things and selfishly decide that she was the source of the rumors. But we've got nothing to do with it. Besides, you don't actually have any proof, do you?"

Ishizaki was clearly frustrated by Hashimoto's words, but Hashimoto wasn't wrong. As of now, there was no conclusive evidence suggesting that it was Sakayanagi who had put the letters in the mailboxes or posted the rumors on the online bulletin boards...even though we knew that in all probability, it was her.

"So that's what today's about. You guys wanted to press me about this whole thing, huh? Gotta say, I had no idea that you Class-D folks had Ichinose's back," said Hashimoto.

Ishizaki and his group glared in response. Hashimoto let out a sigh, as if to show he understood the situation he was in.

"There's no point in trying to fool us. You haven't just been spreadin' crap about Ichinose. You've been makin' up stuff about us too."

"I see. So that's the reason, huh? You don't really care about Ichinose—you just don't like that Class D got caught up in these rumors. Oh, yeah, they said something about you getting put in juvenile detention for a prank you played on an elementary school student. Isn't that right, Ishizaki?"

The moment those words passed Hashimoto's lips, Ishizaki snapped. Hiyori hurriedly grabbed Ishizaki's arm, holding him back before he could pounce on Hashimoto.

The rumor Hashimoto just mentioned was one of the supposed lies posted on the bulletin board. Ishizaki's fury was inevitable, the result of being in a situation like this. Hashimoto, showing no signs of backing down, continued speaking.

"But seriously, I'm amazed that you came up with all of these rumors. Come on, tell me how you managed to sniff out all this stuff about other people, not just Ichinose?"

"Stop screwing with us, Hashimoto!"

"Wait, Ishizaki!"

Akito, thinking that Hiyori wouldn't be able to hold Ishizaki back on her own, hurriedly tried to stop him.

"Don't try to stop me, Miyake! Like hell I'm just gonna sit here and let Class A just keep doing whatever they feel like!! I'm gonna punch his lights out!"

"Knock it off, Ishizaki. You're the one who'll get hurt, understand? You're probably confident in your fighting skills, but I can throw down pretty well myself, you know?" said Kitou, quietly taking one step forward and putting his fists up in a fighting stance, readying himself against Ishizaki and Albert. It looked like he was ready to accept their challenge, should the situation call for it.

"Cut it out, you guys. You all know how mad the school gets when it comes to fights," said Akito, trying to calm things down, while standing at a distance.

"Until now, that is."

"Until now?"

"I've heard that the current student council president is actually willing to tolerate a little bad behavior here and there. Get it?"

Hashimoto closed the distance between himself and Ishizaki, launching his right leg into a kick. Akito blocked it with his left arm.

"Tch... S-seriously? Jeez, seems like anything's possible with this president."

Hashimoto's word alone wasn't enough to convince us the ban on fighting had been lifted. Which was precisely why he'd gone on to prove it by taking the initiative himself.

"Not bad, Miyake. Man, it's no wonder you were so confident when you said you could stop us from fighting," said Hashimoto, taking his distance once again.

The atmosphere became even more tense than it was before. That feeling of pins and needles washed over everyone.

"Fighting is not okay," said Hiyori.

"I know. I didn't come here to fight with you guys. That there was just my way of proving to you that we have the power to defend ourselves," replied Hashimoto.

"...Can we trust you?"

Hashimoto nodded, looking Hiyori in the eyes. And yet, no one believed him.

"Come on, enough already, Hiyori. This guy lies without even batting an eyelash. No matter how you think about it, it was Class A who spread these rumors. The proof is that Class A was the only one not targeted by the rumors."

"But... isn't that also precisely why it's possible that they're not the ones responsible?" said Hiyori.

"It's just like Shiina-chan says," said Hashimoto. "If we were the ones who spread the rumors, wouldn't we have made sure to post something on the Class A bulletin board too, to deflect suspicion?"

"I'm not so sure about that. I can't imagine every student in Class A knows Sakayanagi was the person behind those rumors about Ichinose. If rumors targeting Class A surfaced, it would naturally cause confusion within the class."

After Akito pointed that out, Hashimoto let out a sigh. "Well, I can't really say that your reasoning is off there, to be sure. But it's *probatio diabolica*, isn't it?"

Despite the fact that their actions were extremely suspicious, we had no evidence to prove their guilt. Meanwhile, it was equally difficult for them to prove their innocence.

"The only way we're going to get the truth out of them is if we let our fists do the talking."

"Whoa, hey now. Knock it off, Ibuki-chan. Even if we fight, you're not going to get anything out of it, you know?"

"Telling us to stop after you were just trying to pick a fight with us yourself, huh? You've got a lot of nerve."

"We've got nothing to do with this. Believe me," said Hashimoto, letting out a laugh.

Ibuki, though, wasn't smiling. On the contrary, she seemed to be trying her absolute hardest to hold back her anger. One of the rumors had targeted her, just like Ishizaki.

"You...think you can make fun of us just because Ryuuen quit being our leader, huh?" said Ishizaki.

He must have reached the limits of his patience, because he pushed past Akito. Then, as if moving in lockstep with Ishizaki, Ibuki went to stand in front of Hashimoto and Kitou.

"Wait, wait a second! Seriously!"

"Make Sakayanagi apologize both for the rumors about Ichinose and the rumors about us."

"You've got it wrong. We didn't spread the rumors."

"Stop laughing!"

Ishizaki kicked the railing as hard as he could. Hashimoto was beginning to understand that he couldn't control the situation anymore.

"...Okay, so what're you going to do about it?"

"Ain't that obvious? I'll shut you up by force."

"You seriously think you can do that?"

"Yep. And if you don't want that, then you better go make her take those rumors back, right now."

"I keep telling you, we didn't start those rumors."

Though he kept saying that, Hashimoto understood no one believed him. What Sakayanagi had done was as good as declaring war on Ichinose; it was difficult for him to prove his innocence after such that. His mouth curved back into a smile.

"This ain't something to laugh about."

"Sorry, sorry. It's just that this is just too absurd for me to even comprehend."

Since Hashimoto couldn't admit that Sakayanagi was the source of the rumors, he had no choice but to reject Ishizaki's request.

"In that case, you'll just have to let us talk to Sakayanagi herself."

"You? Yeah, no way," said Hashimoto with a wave of his hand, as if dismissing the very idea that Sakayanagi would meet with them. Ishizaki had to have known it was impossible too, which was why he'd approached Hashimoto. "Kitou. We might not have any other choice."

It seemed Hashimoto, sensing the mood, had decided words were no longer going to work. Kitou, who'd been preparing himself for this, assumed a fighting stance right after.

"Hah!" shouted Ishizaki, rushing at Kitou, attempting to tackle him. Right beside him, Ibuki delivered a flying kick at Hashimoto, which he rushed to avoid in a panic.

"Christ!" shouted Hashimoto.

Because of her powerful jump, Ibuki's cell phone and student ID card fell out of her pocket and hit the ground.

Realizing she was faster and stronger than he'd imagined, Hashimoto's expression showed that he sensed the danger he was in.

"Wow, you're much more used to fighting than I remember, Ibuki-chan..." he said, expressing his respect. "Guess I forgot about that."

"Stop it, everyone!" shouted Akito, picking up the cell phone that lay on the ground nearby.

However, the Class-D students showed no signs of stopping. Ibuki didn't seem at all fazed that her phone might be damaged. I reached out and grabbed her student ID, which had fallen near my feet, lowered my eyes without thinking to read it. Naturally, she wasn't smiling in the picture. She had her usual brusque, stiff expression on her face.

However...one particular detail caught my eye.

"What does this mean...?" I muttered aloud.

"What?" asked Keisei, apparently having heard what I had mumbled from beside him. I quickly shook my head to dismiss the question and put Ibuki's student ID card in my pocket for the time being, for safe-keeping.

"Oh, it's nothing. More importantly, our biggest priority is stopping this fight."

"Stopping it...? How?"

The fight had already turned into a two-versus-two situation, and it looked like round two was about to begin.

"He's right, we should stay out of it."

"It looks dangerous, Kiyotaka-kun..."

Haruka and Airi spoke up, saying that we should stay out of it.

"...I suppose you're right. Leaving it to Akito is probably the wise choice," I replied.

Akito intervened to try to stop the next assault.

"Don't get in the way, Miyake!"

Ishizaki attempted to shove him out of the way with brute force, but Akito grabbed his hand and forcefully pushed Ishizaki down.

"Hey, you jerk, let go!"

"Sorry, Ishizaki. I don't hate guys like you or anything, but I gotta stop you."

"Back off!" shouted Ibuki, aiming a kick at Akito's head.

Akito hurriedly moved away from Ishizaki, just barely dodging Ibuki's foot by the skin of his teeth, but he lost his balance in the process. Albert then grabbed Akito with his large arms.

"Hold him, Albert."

"Gr..."

There was no way for Akito to break free of Albert's monstrously strong grip. Class D had determined that they wouldn't lose as long as they managed to keep this fight two-on-two.

"Ibuki!" shouted Ishizaki. At the same time, Kitou thrust his hand forward, aiming at Ibuki's neck.

"Don't underestimate me!" shouted Ibuki, reacting to Kitou's attack by kicking his hand away.

"They're going at it for real... What do we do?"

The four of us watched, unable to stop them.

"Well, nothing we can really do about it now, since the fight's started, but you Class-C guys are really in the way here..." Hashimoto looked over at us, still keeping an eye on Ishizaki, who had just gotten back up.

"We happened to come here by coincidence, but there is something that we'd like to say. One of our friends... Ayanokouji has been targeted and affected by these rumors, just like Ishizaki and the others," said Keisei. When he appealed to Hashimoto, Airi, who was standing next to him, nodded enthusiastically.

"Oh? Oh, yeah, there was something about him, wasn't there? A lovely little rumor about him having a crush on Karuizawa or something, right?"

"I-It's absolutely not lovely at all!" said the usually soft-spoken Airi, raising her voice to object, which was a rare sight.

Going along with them, I addressed Hashimoto as well. "I hate to say this, but I suspect you too, Hashimoto."

"...Guess that makes sense. I mean, I was the only one who saw you and Karuizawa meeting in secret the other day, after all."

"M-meeting in secret?"

Not just Airi, but Haruka quickly turned around to look at me too.

"There's nothing strange going on between us at all," I said.

"Really? B-but, Kiyotaka-kun, I have gotten the impression that you and Karuizawa-san have been getting along pretty well lately..." said Airi.

Well, Airi did watch me very carefully, so it wasn't surprising she'd seen that much. But the important thing was that Hashimoto heard her say that. I needed him to know that there were other people who were aware of the kind of relationship I had with Kei. There needed to be the appearance of a certain degree of intimacy between me and Kei if the excuse we'd used the other day—that I was the middleman, delivering chocolates on Kei's behalf to her real crush—was to appear legitimate.

Hashimoto was doing this to ascertain how my classmates saw my relationship with Kei. But it was precisely his own cleverness that would cause him to end up closing himself off to several possibilities. Even though he'd been keeping his eyes on me, he was going to draw out testimony that suggested I posed no threat to him. As a result, his suspicions of me would fade.

"I'm your opponent right now, Hashimoto!"

"Come on, dude... This is getting to be really annoying."

"Please Ishizaki-kun, stop! Don't do this anymore! At the very least, I cannot allow this," said Hiyori, speaking in a firm tone.

Ishizaki, unable to ignore her, looked back at her with a troubled expression.

"B-but!"

"Even if you do manage to beat Hashimoto-kun and Kitou-kun in a fight and force them to confess, that won't amount to real evidence. The person at the heart of the matter, Sakayanagi-san, still won't admit to anything. Isn't it enough that we couldn't get them to confess?" said Hiyori.

"So you're telling Ibuki and me to just shut up and take it?"

"I know that is going to sound harsh, but yes. Please bear with it for now."

"You're the one who asked us to come with you, aren't you? And yet you're telling us to bear with it? That doesn't make any sense!"

"I promise that I'll make it up to you," said Hiyori.

Hashimoto let out a whistle, seemingly deeply inter-ested in what he just heard. "Oh, ho, so it wasn't Ishizaki who set up this meeting, but you, Shiina-chan?"

"Albert-kun. Please let him go."

Albert slowly released Akito, as instructed.

"We've really caused you guys from Class C a lot of trouble," said Hiyori, bowing deeply.

"Wow, okay, you think this is all over, just like that? Talk about one-sided. So what, you accuse us, try to beat us up, and we're just supposed to accept it?"

"Could you please forgive us?"

Hashimoto accepted what Hiyori had to say. He must have known that there was nothing to be gained by pushing the issue. "Well, it's not like we're injured or anything. Let's call it a day then, Kitou. But please, stop single-mindedly blaming us. If you must accuse us, find some ironclad proof first, okay?"

Somehow, Hiyori had successfully managed to bring the situation under control before it devolved into an all-out brawl. However, the relationship between Class A and the other classes had now deteriorated to the point where it was impossible to repair.

7.7

∙ ∙

THAT NIGHT, I called Horikita Manabu.

"It's rather unusual for me to get a call from you," said Horikita.

"There's one thing I want to ask you."

"What is it?"

I reported what I'd noticed after looking at two students' ID cards.

"I hope that this isn't just a misunderstanding on your part," answered Horikita, sounding surprised, as if this was the first he'd heard of this.

"Based on your reaction, I'm guessing the student council... no, I mean that this has never happened before?" I asked.

"That's correct. That is, as long as it's not just some simple mistake."

I couldn't exclude the possibility that it was a mistake, of course. But if it was, it was a very rare one.

"The school changes and evolves every year. This phenomenon, too, should have some meaning. As I'm quite possibly the first person to have noticed it, a day may come when it will prove useful to you."

Even if that day came, I hoped I could wrap things up without having to make use of it, if at all possible.

"You first-year students will likely have one more special exam to complete this year," Horikita said.

I made note of the fact that he referenced the first-years specifically. Did that mean the situation was different for us?

"Well, that's the way it's been in previous years, at least. I can't be absolutely certain it'll be that way this year. But if things proceed as they have in the past, even the third-year students should be facing two or more special exams," added Horikita.

"So it's going to be quite the rough time for you, huh?" If all the second-year students led by Nagumo put their weight behind the students of third-year Class B, then Horikita's position was by no means safe.

"It's a highly unpredictable situation, that's for sure. But it's nothing that you need to be concerned about."

As I'd expect of the former student council president.

He didn't seem to consider his current situation hopeless, and I felt confident he had the strength to fight his way through.

However, my confidence was in Horikita Manabu, and Horikita Manabu alone. Just like he'd targeted Tachibana Akane, I was sure that Nagumo would take aim at other victims whom he could break down.

"What you should be worried about now is the first-year class as a whole," said Horikita.

"If the student council is backing him, then Nagumo should be able to sweep whatever he wants under the rug," I reasoned.

"Yes, that's possible. Of course, the student council might lose the school's trust and be forcibly disbanded if they go too far...but we're dealing with Nagumo here. He'll probably handle things quite cleverly. Did you have any trouble with that matter regarding Kushida?"

"Oh, that's been taken care of."

"It seems there's been a lot happening behind the scenes where this whole ordeal with Ichinose is concerned."

"I'll contact you again."

Having ascertained what I wanted to know, I ended the call.

7.8

THE NEXT FEW DAYS passed by in a flash. Ichinose, the center of this whirlwind of controversy, continued to be absent until February 24th, one day before the year-end final exam, when she finally returned to class. I didn't see her myself, but there were a lot of people tracking her every move with watchful eyes because she hadn't been to class in over a week's time. News about her return reached me almost immediately.

That being said, this was only really important to Class B. Class C was far more occupied with the year-end final exam awaiting us tomorrow.

"All right. Ayanokouji, Akito, Haruka, and Airi, you all did great."

During our lunch break, we gathered around Keisei's desk. We'd taken a mock test that Keisei had prepared for us to take independently, at night, in order to test our abilities. And he'd just got done grading our answers.

"Whoa, Kiyopon, you got 90 points? That's awesome!" said Haruka, sounding surprised, as she ate her sandwich.

"Well, that's because the tests that Keisei made for us are perfect. You got a good score too, didn't you?" Though their scores varied a little, the three of them had all scored in the neighborhood of 80 points.

"Well, if you managed to get through both the practice test and the mock test that I made, then I'm sure you should do fine in the test tomorrow," said Keisei.

"If you're giving us the seal of approval, Keisei, then I'm sure it'll be a piece of cake," said Akito, rolling his stiff shoulders, as if squaring up to fight.

"Really, thank you so much, Keisei-kun. I always get so anxious every time I take a test..." said Airi.

"Oh, no need to thank me. This is the least I can do," said Keisei. He lightly scratched the bridge of his nose, looking a little embarrassed.

"Is it really okay if we take the rest of the day off?"

"You've spent a lot of time studying this week. Honestly, I think it's a good idea to take it easy on this last day. It's not like everything you've studied so carefully will just slip away so soon. Besides, you don't want to overdo it now and get sick, or end up falling asleep on the day of the exam. It would be a real shame if you lose points over such a trivial mistake."

"Roger! I'll follow your orders, Yukimuu!" replied Haruka, offering Keisei a bizarre salute. The others nodded along, sharing her same sentiment.

Bam!

Suddenly, a loud sound echoed throughout the classroom. It was the sound of the door being violently flung open.

"Whoa! You guys! This is huge!"

Just as we were about to casually enjoy the rest of our lunch too. Talk about bad timing.

"Ugh, seriously?" Haruka, startled, had accidentally dropped her sandwich on the floor. She glared at Ike, clearly mad and not trying to hide it. "Hey! What's your deal?!"

"Dude, it's like a mob! Like pitchforks and everything! A bunch of Class A people are marching into Class B right now!" shouted Ike excitedly.

"So Sakayanagi-san is making her move now that Ichinose-san has returned, huh..." said Horikita, who'd also been eating lunch in the classroom. She stood up quickly, looking disturbed, and left the classroom without saying anything to me.

Seeing her leave, Sudou, Hirata, and a few others followed. Tomorrow was the year-end exam. If Sakayanagi was going to end this, today was the last chance she'd have. She intended to launch a direct assault on Ichinose right after she'd returned and finish her off.

"What should we do, Akito...?"

"We have no choice but to head over there. If it turns out like what happened the other day, then someone has to be there to stop it."

"Yeah, that makes sense."

"But Haruka, Airi, you two stay here. There's no point in getting more people involved."

"Yeah, yeah, we get it. We'll take our time eating."

"What are you going to do, Kiyotaka-kun?"

"I—"

Keisei had risen to his feet, along with Akito. It would be hard for me to say I was staying behind, in a situation like this.

"I'll go too, just in case. Though I don't think I'll be much help."

The three of us left the classroom and headed toward Class B. The commotion seemed to have already spilled out into the hallway, and there was an obvious crowd forming.

"What did you come here for, Sakayanagi?!" As we entered Class B, we heard Shibata shout.

"What did I come here for? I've come to rescue all of you in Class B. Don't you see?"

Sakayanagi was accompanied by Kamuro and Hashimoto, though I saw no sign of Kitou or anyone else. They'd probably have gotten more pushback if they showed up in greater numbers, which was why they'd chosen to take action with a small group.

"What do you mean by that, Sakayanagi?" asked Ichinose, speaking up from the back of the classroom where she stood surrounded by several students.

"Wait, Ichinose. There's no need for you to get involved."

"Yeah, that's right, Honami-chan. Don't go!"

One of the students hugged Ichinose tightly, trying to prevent her from going to see Sakayanagi.

"First of all, I must say I'm quite glad to see that you've made a full recovery. To be honest, I wanted to speak to you much earlier, but I've been *ever* so busy studying for the exam. Ah, but yes, I'm glad to see you're back. Just in time for the year-end exam, too."

"Yes. Thank you."

They spoke to each other across the classroom. It was clear to see that every student in Class B considered

Sakayanagi a foe. Even though it was lunch break, there wasn't a single student missing from the class. They'd all decided to stick together to protect Ichinose.

However, Sakayanagi didn't appear shaken at all. If anything, she seemed to be enjoying the feeling of being deep in enemy territory. She must have anticipated that Ichinose, who was still caught at the center of a whirlwind of controversy, wouldn't have gone somewhere like the school cafeteria during her lunch break.

"You say you came here to save us, Sakayanagi?" asked Kanzaki.

"Yes," replied Sakayanagi with a smile and a nod.

"Does that mean you're admitting that you started those rumors? I suppose I can understand how you'd be 'saving us' if you came here to apologize."

"I am not the one who started the rumors," she replied.

"...Then what are you saving us from, exactly?"

"Do you recall a rumor that went around earlier? The one about how Ichinose-san had accumulated a massive number of points? At the time, the school had declared that no wrongdoing had taken place, and the matter was quickly put to rest."

"What about it?" replied Kanzaki without a second's delay, moving fast to keep Ichinose from saying anything.

"Now, this might just be my imagination, but... Well, there are only a few ways that someone could collect that many points without resorting to illegal means. One of those ways would be to collect private points from your classmates on a regular basis and hold onto them. In short, I've determined that Ichinose is acting as something of a banker for your class."

"I can't really say anything about that," said Kanzaki.

If true, it was part of Class B's strategy. It was only natural he'd deny knowing anything.

"I suppose so. Well, it's not like I really came here seeking an answer on that matter. It's just... Well, it's just that if Ichinose-san is playing the role of a banker, as I have surmised, then...I think that's extremely dangerous for all of you," said Sakayanagi, looking over at Ichinose, who returned her gaze from afar.

"............"

Ichinose didn't answer. Instead, she simply continued to look straight back at Sakayanagi.

"Is what I've said incorrect? Ichinose Honami-san?"

A cruel situation, Sakayanagi. You've certainly cornered Ichinose.

Ichinose, who'd had no weapon but silence at her disposal so far, had been driven to the edge of a cliff. One final push would send her plummeting to the bottom.

It was precisely the situation Sakayanagi had worked to create.

However, her plan wasn't going to work.

"Sorry, but Chihiro-chan, Mako-chan, could you give me a little space?" asked Ichinose.

"B-but!"

"It's okay. I'll be just fine. You don't have to worry anymore," said Ichinose with a gentle smile, as she slowly closed the distance between herself and Sakayanagi.

In the end, however, she didn't move to face Sakayanagi directly. Instead, she took up a position at the teacher's podium, facing all of her classmates.

"...I'm sorry!" said Ichinose, bowing her head before all of the students of Class B.

"Wh-what are you apologizing to us for, Ichinose? There's no reason for you to apologize to us. Right?" said Shibata, clearly upset, trying to stop Ichinose from speaking.

"Please don't try to stop her, Shibata-kun. She's just trying to repent," said Sakayanagi, smiling merrily.

"The whole year I've been here... There's a secret that I've been keeping hidden from you. I've been keeping it for a long, long time."

"Wait, Ichinose. You don't need to say anything here," said Kanzaki, clearly sensing that something was amiss. But Ichinose wasn't stopping.

"There have been quite a few strange rumors circulating about me these past few weeks. However, one of those rumors is actually the truth. Just as that letter said... I am a criminal."

As Ichinose spoke those words, Sakayanagi wore a satisfied smile on her face.

"Is that really true?"

The noisy classroom once again fell silent.

"It would seem this group of good-natured souls have absolutely no idea what's going on here, so please do give them all the details, Ichinose-san. Exactly what kind of crime did you commit?"

"I—"

Ichinose was about to continue speaking, but she stopped and gulped nervously.

"I've been keeping secrets from all of you...but I'm going to confess everything, starting now," she finally said, revealing the past she'd kept buried. "The crime that I've been silent about... Well, it's that I was a shoplifter."

The shoplifting honor student, Ichinose Honami. It was a revelation that didn't only surprise Class B, but also the spectators on the sidelines, like Akito and Keisei. Ichinose just didn't seem like the kind of person who'd do such a thing.

"Honami-chan is... a shoplifter...? I-Is that true?"

"Yes. I'm sorry, Mako-chan."

As she apologized to everyone, Ichinose started to tell us the story of how it started.

"I came from a single-parent family. My father wasn't in the picture, so I lived with my mom and my two younger sisters. We weren't wealthy, but we were never unhappy. My mother always seemed like she had it so hard, raising my two younger sisters while working. That was why, when I was in elementary school, I got the idea to start working myself once I graduated from junior high. It did cost a lot of money to go to high school, after all. I thought I'd get a job, help my mom out, help support my two younger sisters. But my mom was strongly against the idea. Just as I wanted my younger sisters to be happy, my mom, too, wished for her daughters' happiness," said Ichinose, telling us about everything that happened in her past.

"I learned that even if you were poor, you could benefit from a scholarship if you studied really hard for it. So I studied as hard as I possibly could. I studied so much that I got to the level where I was told that I was number one in my whole school. But...in the summer of my third year of junior high...my mother worked herself too hard and collapsed."

Ichinose's mother must have been working hard to support her family. She'd worked herself to the bone to raise her children.

"My little sister's birthday was coming up. She'd never once asked me or our mother for a gift before. She was still only in her first year of junior high. She deserved to have us spoil her a little, but she never asked us for anything. Not for clothes that she wanted, or to go hang out with friends or go shopping...all she did was endure, never asking for anything. She always, always, always held back.

"But then, for the first time...my little sister said that there was something she wanted. It was this kind of hair clip that used to be really popular, something that my sister's favorite celebrity wore. I'm sure my mom pushed herself harder, picking up extra shifts, just so she could buy it."

And instead, she'd been hospitalized. From the sound of it, she hadn't been able to get her daughter the birthday present she wanted.

"Even now, I still remember the sight of my little sister's face, as she shouted and screamed all kinds of things at our mother, who was crying and apologizing to her from her hospital bed. I remember watching her shout and cry about how she'd been looking forward to getting that hair clip. I couldn't even really blame her for acting like that. It was the only gift she had ever asked for..." said Ichinose.

The smile never faded from Sakayanagi's face as she continued to listen to Ichinose's confession.

"As her older sister... I thought I had to bring back my little sister's smile, whatever it took. So, on the day of my sister's birthday, after class, I went to the department store."

I was sure that Ichinose's heart was racing nervously right now, just like it had back then.

"I'm sure I was burying my real feelings, back then. I told myself it was okay. That it wasn't a big deal to do something bad like this, just this one time, for my sister's sake. After all, there were plenty of people who did bad things in the world. Why should my family, who'd put up with so much for so long, be blamed? I told myself what I was doing could be forgiven. That was the selfish, self-centered justification I gave myself."

Ichinose's words came forth as if she were releasing something heavy she'd been holding onto.

"That hair clip cost ten thousand yen or more. So...I stole it. I stole the hair clip that my little sister wanted. It was an act that made everyone unhappy. But at that time, all I wanted was to make my sister happy, somehow."

And that act triggered what followed.

"...But it doesn't matter, does it?" muttered Ichinose quietly. She kept going, stringing together disconnected phrases in an attempt to express her jumbled thoughts.

"Ultimately, a crime is a crime. No matter how much you repent, your sins will never disappear."

"So you're saying that you got caught?" asked Hashimoto. Ichinose simply shook her head.

"I just left the department store with the hair clip. It was the first time I'd ever shoplifted. The first time I ever committed a crime, at all. No one saw me. I went back home and gave it to my little sister, who was still moping around. I'd just stolen it, so it wasn't wrapped or anything. It was such a sloppy gift. But she was so incredibly happy to see it. When I saw her smile, I felt my guilt fade away for a moment. But it didn't fade entirely. It came back and continued to grow and grow inside me."

Ichinose let out a chuckle of self-derision.

"I mean, there's absolutely no way a mother wouldn't notice when her own daughter did something bad, right? I told my sister to keep the gift a secret. But she wore it when we went to visit our mother in the hospital. I mean, of course she would. She could never have dreamed it was a stolen gift. That was the first time in my life that I ever saw my mother seriously angry. She slapped me and took the gift from my crying little sister, who didn't understand. Even though she should have still been in the hospital, my mother dragged me all the way back to the store, where I got on my knees and begged for forgiveness. That was when I finally understood the weight of my crime. I realized that no matter what excuses I made, there was nothing I could do to take it all back."

That was Ichinose's past. The past she had been hiding.

"In the end, the clerk at the store didn't hand me over to the police. Still, word got out. In the blink of an eye, my family was the center of controversy. I shut down and retreated inward. For almost half my third year of junior high, I cut myself off from the world and stayed in my room... But eventually, I started thinking about trying to move forward, once again. It was my homeroom teacher telling me about this school back then that made me start to think about it. You were exempted from paying tuition fees and course fees, and if you graduated, you could get a job anywhere. I wanted to start over. I wanted a fresh slate."

As Ichinose had finished telling her story, she bowed once more to all of the students in Class B.

"I'm sorry, everyone. I'm such a pathetic, useless leader..."

"That's not true, Ichinose," said Shibata, who had been listening nearby. "I heard everything you had to say, and I still think that you're a good person. I'm sure of it. Right?"

"Yeah. You might have done something bad, Honami-chan, but—"

Klak!

The loud crack of a cane being struck against the floor echoed throughout the room.

"Please, spare me. Could you Class-B cretins at least *try* to not make me laugh?" said Sakayanagi, curtly brushing aside the voices coming out in support of Ichinose. "Really, this is such an absurd farce. Do you mean to gain sympathy by bringing up unnecessary details about your past? No matter the circumstances, shoplifting is still shoplifting. You don't deserve sympathy. Your thievery was for the sake of your own self-interest."

Standing nearby, Kamuro's expression stiffened for a moment as she heard what Sakayanagi said.

"Yes, you're absolutely right. The circumstances of my past don't make any difference at all," said Ichinose.

"The truth of the matter is that you *committed a crime*. Therefore, isn't it fair to assume you might also steal the large quantity of private points that you've been entrusted with, around the time graduation draws near?" said Sakayanagi.

"...I could never do something like that, Sakayanagi-san. If I ignored everyone else's wishes and moved up to Class A myself, it would be an act of betrayal. I don't think the school would allow something like that either," said Ichinose.

"Yes, I suppose so. You *are* rather clever, so I suppose you wouldn't do something so obvious. But what if you were to, for example, put on a show for everyone? Give a little speech to earn everyone's sympathy, like you just did, to gain their approval to move on up to Class A?" said Sakayanagi, relentlessly pressing the attack.

"Yes, you have a point. Maybe... Maybe no matter how hard I try, my efforts will just come off as hypocritical. Once you've committed a crime, it can never be erased."

Ichinose would always be stuck with the label of a criminal, and that label meant people would never stop suspecting that she might eventually betray them one day.

"Do you all understand now, everyone? This is the real Ichinose Honami-san. As long as you have such a person as your leader, Class B has no chance of victory," said Sakayanagi, driving home the reality of the situation. "Now, please return all your private points to these students, and step down as the leader of Class B. I would like for you to do at least that much. If you don't, these awful rumors about you will never stop, will they?"

Ichinose closed her eyes. Then, quietly, she took a deep breath.

"So what do you say, Ichinose? What do you want to do?" asked Kanzaki, representing Class B.

The question was whether or not she would continue as the class leader. Ichinose, and only Ichinose, was the one who could make that decision. If this had been the first time she'd had her spirit crushed, then maybe she wouldn't have held firm. Maybe she would have submitted.

However, Ichinose had already had her spirit broken before.

And I was the one who'd broken it.

But she had recovered. The parts of her that had been broken had become stronger and more resilient than before.

"This is the end of my penitence!" said Ichinose, turning to Sakayanagi with a smile. "It is certainly true that I shoplifted. As you said, Sakayanagi-san, I don't deserve sympathy. A crime is a crime, after all. I have no intention of running from that truth. But the truth is that I was never given a sentence to serve out for that crime. In other words, what's done is done. I don't need to keep paying the price."

"What an incredibly shameless thing to say. You're being unbelievably bold, for a shoplifting thief."

"Maybe so. But I'm not looking back anymore. I won't let my past keep me down." Ichinose turned her smiling face toward her classmates. "Even though I'm so shameless... Will you follow me until the end, everyone?"

After she spoke, there was a moment of silence. Ichinose wasn't speaking from a false sense of confidence or optimism. Even now, she was on the verge of tears. She wanted to run away. She was ashamed of her past. And yet, she continued to push forward. There was no way the students of Class B, who'd shared a year of joys and sorrows with her, wouldn't understand that.

"Well, of course we'll follow you! Right?!" shouted Shibata, with a smile.

Every single student of Class B let out a unanimous cheer. This was the kind of following Ichinose inspired. I could really feel the depth of their devotion to her. Keisei and Akito beamed, seeming similarly overjoyed by this showing of support from Class B.

I doubted there was a single other student at this school who could inspire this kind of support. Ichinose wasn't just being cheered on by the entirety of Class B, but by students from other classes too.

"Sakayanagi... What do we do now?" asked Kamuro.

Sakayanagi's attack had been neutralized. Kamuro could tell, which was why she spoke up, asking a question that could be interpreted as her subtly suggesting that they retreat.

"Heh heh heh." Sakayanagi laughed. "Heh heh heh heh."

Then she laughed again, a little longer this time.

"I see. Well, it would appear you've pulled the wool quite adeptly over your classmates' eyes. But as you said yourself earlier, it's not as though your criminal past will just disappear. Rumors will continue to spread about you for a long, long time to come," said Sakayanagi.

"Yes. But I'm not going to run away from it anymore."

"Is that so? Why then, I'm just going to have to thoroughly des—"

"Okay, that's quite enough, everyone."

Just as Sakayanagi was about to answer Ichinose, some teachers and students entered Class B. The new arrivals were Student Council President Nagumo, as well as the homeroom teacher for Class B, Hoshinomiya, and our homeroom teacher, Chabashira.

"Oh my, this is quite an impressive gathering. However, this is a matter between the first-year students, is it not?" asked Sakayanagi.

"You're correct that this appears to be a dispute between first-years, sure. However, as of today, the act of carelessly spreading rumors is prohibited," Nagumo told her.

"...What do you mean? I don't accept the imposition of such a gag order. Regardless of how the rumors about her originated, if Ichinose-san was troubled by them, she should have reported them to the school, no?"

"That's not it, Sakayanagi. This is no longer just about Ichinose," replied Nagumo.

"...What are you saying?"

Nagumo opened his mouth to explain, but Chabashira spoke up instead.

"I won't go into detail, but it has been clearly confirmed that slanderous statements are being exchanged between the first-year students," she explained. "There are already close to twenty rumors in circulation. Any further gossip will damage social bonds and negatively impact student behavior. Rumors are rumors, but regardless of whether they can be conclusively proven true or false, the school no longer wishes to see the spread of rumors targeting specific individuals. Therefore, I'm taking this opportunity to inform you that, going forward, anyone who circulates nonsensical rumors may be punished for their actions."

The school had been silently tolerating the endless rumor-mongering so far. It seemed they'd finally decided to take action.

"...I see. So that's how it is, then," said Sakayanagi, appearing to understand the situation after hearing Chabashira's explanation.

"I suppose this means the school is finally taking a stand," Horikita said to me. She'd approached to get a good look at the situation, and similarly grasped what was going on. "I suppose this might be enough to save the affected classes. As for Ichinose-san, the original target of all of this...I don't think Sakayanagi's faction can keep attacking her. The rumors about Hondou-kun, Shinohara-san, you, and Satou-san should be put to rest now too."

"Yeah, I suppose so."

"Sakayanagi-san went too far. She tried to use the same strategy to attack all the other classes at the same time, but in doing so, her movements became too conspicuous and drew the school's attention. It seems this was just an overzealous move from an incredibly aggressive girl," said Horikita.

After saying that, she fell silent. Then, a short while later, she opened her mouth to speak again.

"But—"

"What's up?"

"Never mind. It's nothing."

Horikita didn't seem to want to say any more.

"Let's pull back. If the school's making its move, then I believe that our presence is no longer required here."

Sakayanagi, understanding what was going on, gave the order to her classmates to withdraw. The uproarious Class B grew even louder, in celebration. Class A had been completely driven back.

7.9

WHEN WE MADE IT BACK to Class C, Haruka excitedly asked Akito about what happened.

"Hey, so how was Class B? It sounded like there was this huge commotion over there."

"Things took a completely unexpected turn. Ichinose got Sakayanagi to retreat," said Akito, giving a concise account of what happened with Class B. He told her truth regarding the gossip about Ichinose, and the fact that the school had given us an official notice that spreading rumors would no longer be tolerated from this point on.

"The teachers will probably give us an official statement during afternoon classes."

"Still, shoplifting, huh? I mean, that's super surprising, but I guess it kind of makes what happened next make sense. If people keep bringing up something from your past that you don't want to revisit, then of course you'd wanna take some time off school," said Haruka, speaking out in Ichinose's defense now that she'd learned what happened.

"Anyway, the ordeal is over now. Now let's not get distracted by the rumors and just focus on the exam."

"Isn't this great, Kiyopon?"

"Yeah... I guess so."

Then, my phone rang.

"Who's that from?"

"It's from an unregistered number."

I showed the number displayed on the screen to Haruka and the others. It was a different number than the one I had gotten a call from in the middle of the night, some time ago. I got up from my seat, put a little distance between myself and the rest of the group, and answered the call.

"Hello?"

"Is this Ayanokouji-kun?"

I recognized the caller's voice immediately. It was Sakayanagi. "How did you know my numb—well, I guess it's not too difficult to look up, come to think of it."

"Quite. We still have roughly ten minutes before our lunch break ends. Would you mind stepping outside to meet me?"

I could refuse, but then I'd have to make time to meet up with her later, and that would be a pain. "Where do you want me to go?" I asked, stepping out into the hallway.

"Let's see. How about by the first-floor entryway?" she asked.

"Got it."

I ended the call and made my way over to the entryway. I'd thought that Kamuro and Hashimoto might have been with her, but Sakayanagi was alone when I arrived.

"Please relax. I did not bring anyone with me this time. I must say, you truly performed excellently, Ayanokouji-kun."

"What are you talking about?"

"It would seem you've been working behind the scenes without me noticing. While a number of mysteries remain, I'm not really interested in seeking to solve them. There's only one thing I'm truly curious to know. Why did you decide to protect Ichinose-san?" she asked, her gaze fixated on me.

"Hold on. I have no clue what you're on about."

"I can only imagine that it was precisely because you saved her that Ichinose-san was so bold back then... No, that she was able to get back on her feet again. Perhaps that wasn't the first time she'd confessed what happened in her past? Maybe she's already told someone else about it beforehand?" asked Sakayanagi.

"And that someone else is me, I'm guessing?" I asked.

"Yes."

It was a completely understandable conclusion for her to arrive at.

"Didn't you use Kamuro to make me make a move?" I asked.

"Used Kamuro-san?"

"Before I could seek to clarify the facts myself, she told me everything. Only me. About the fact that Ichinose shoplifted in the past."

"She acted entirely on her own," said Sakayanagi.

"No, that's not true."

"How can you be so sure of that?" Apparently, she wanted to hear my reasoning.

"She handed over a can of beer as proof that she shoplifted. But she hadn't stolen it that day. Kamuro had stolen it on the day she had started school here."

"And what's your basis for saying that?"

"The sell-by date. After I checked the sell-by date on the can of beer that Kamuro handed me, I went over to the convenience store and checked the dates on their stock of the same brand. They were more than four months apart. I find it hard to believe the store happened to have one can that was four months older than the others. Kamuro said that she'd given you the can of beer she stole back then, and that you'd told her you would dispose of it. Which means she re-procured that can from you before meeting me and presented me with it. Or contacted you right after she left my room and got it then."

By that point, the fact of Kamuro contacting me and telling me about Ichinose's past was well within the range of what I had expected.

"Why would you think I'd take such roundabout action?" Sakayanagi asked.

"To lure me out, probably?" I countered.

"Heh heh heh. I suppose I should respond by saying that's just what I'd expect from you, Ayanokouji-kun."

"It would have been easy for me to sit on the sidelines and watch events unfold. Actually, that's exactly what I had planned to do."

The person who made me stray from those plans was none other than Sakayanagi herself. She'd attached Ichinose with one hand, while offering her support with the other. Of course, she'd done the latter in an extremely roundabout way.

"It was all for the sake of getting your attention, Ayanokouji-kun." Sakayanagi, gripping her cane tight, slowly walked toward me. "I didn't care if Ichinose-san was destroyed as a result. However, I was hoping that if I simply left the possibility open for you to intervene, then you would take hold of it. I estimated the odds were fifty-fifty that you would...but it would seem things turned out exactly as I hoped it would."

In other words, she was saying Ichinose's existence didn't matter to her at all.

"Please have a little contest with me, Ayanokouji-kun."

"And if I say no?"

"While you might try to say it wouldn't significantly hurt you, I'd expose you as the mastermind leading Class C. And I'm sure that you understand quite well that that wouldn't be something you could dismiss as a mere rumor."

I was sure Sakayanagi would calmly and unhesitatingly proceed to make my secrets known to all, even if the school had ostensibly prohibited her from spreading rumors.

"So what do you say? Will you accept?" she asked.

"How would we win this? You're Class A. I'm Class C. The difference is obvious."

"Well, I don't know exactly what the next exam will cover, but how about we compare our rankings? If you win, then I promise that from this point on, I will not speak a word to anyone about your past."

While that wasn't a bad offer, there was no guarantee that she was going to honor her word. And I had absolutely no intention of keeping any written or audio records of this arrangement.

"You don't believe me, hm? But you have no choice but to believe me. If you don't, then your past will be exposed for all to see. That would make it rather hard for you to live an ordinary life, wouldn't it?"

"Do whatever you want. If that does happen, though, you'll never, ever get the chance to fight me."

"Heh heh. Yes, I suppose that's what you would say, Ayanokouji-kun."

Sakayanagi knew I wouldn't agree to compete with her so easily. Which was exactly why she had yet to tell anyone about my past.

"Well, then, what if I wager my future at this school? If I lose, I'll drop out. Furthermore, I don't mind if you have my father, the principal, be a witness to act as guarantor." Sakayanagi radiated absolute confidence that she would undoubtedly win against me. "Of course, even if you lose to me, there's no need for you to leave the school. I don't intend to ask you to wager anything significant, either. I will, however, publicly announce that you are the mastermind leading Class C. That is all. If you won't accept some degree of risk, then you might simply withdraw from our little contest."

"If those are your conditions, then I accept."

"Thank you very much, Ayanokouji-kun. It seems my boring life here at this school is finally at an end."

With a broad, satisfied grin on her face, Sakayanagi withdrew.

I decided to call the person at the center of recent events; the one who'd been looming in the background the whole time. It wasn't Horikita, or Kei. And not Horikita's brother either.

"I was just thinking it was about time I heard from you. Good evening, Ayanokouji-kun."

8 ALL THE TRICKS

THIS PART OF THE STORY went back to Friday, February 11th. The day when those letters stating Ichinose was a criminal were dropped in our mailboxes. After seeing Ichinose be affected by them, and having Kamuro get in touch with me to talk about her past as a shoplifter, I decided to lay out my pieces in advance so I'd be prepared for Sakayanagi's strategy.

To execute that plan, I called a certain female student on her phone and asked her to come and meet me in my room.

The time of our meeting arrived, and I heard the sound of light knocking on my door, rather than the doorbell. Since the door was already unlocked, I simply opened it. The faint scent of flowers tickled my nose at the same time that I felt the cold air rush in from the hallway.

"Good evening, Ayanokouji-kun." Since it was around midnight, Kushida spoke in a lowered tone.

"Sorry for calling you at such a late hour. If you don't mind, please come on in."

"Are you sure?"

"It'd be cold if we stayed out by the front door, wouldn't it?" I replied.

"Yes, that's true. Thank you."

Going into a boy's room in the middle of the night. And being alone together, on top of that. Anyone would find the idea fishy, but Kushida had come to my room without any hesitation.

"It's a little early, but this is for you, Ayanokouji-kun."

She took out a box of chocolates that had been wrapped with a pink ribbon. She must have been keeping it inside her jacket.

"You're okay with giving me this?" I asked.

"I have quite a few to give out on the 14th, so if there's anyone I can give them to early, I've been doing just that."

Since that was the case, I accepted them graciously. There was no reason for me to refuse.

"So then, what did you want to talk to me about? It's rather unusual for you to call at this time of night." If this were a casual conversation, I could've approached her in the morning or afternoon. It was natural for her to be suspicious.

"There's something I want to discuss with you."

"Hm..." Kushida sounded surprised. "I thought you hated me, Ayanokouji-kun. And that you wouldn't want to discuss anything with me."

"I don't really hate you. Actually, if anything, I thought you'd prefer to avoid me. Right?"

"Ah ha ha ha! I see, well, I suppose you're right about that."

The laugh she released wasn't that of the persona she showed everyone else, but it wasn't a true reflection of the self she hid underneath either. It was something in between.

"But don't you have Horikita-san? Isn't she far more reliable than someone like me?" she asked.

"I can't rely on anyone but you for this, Kushida."

"Well, I don't really know if I can be of much help, but I don't mind hearing you out, at least. But what do you mean when you say I'm the only one who can help you?" she asked, tilting her head to the side in apparent confusion.

"I want personal information about some first-year students that would embarrass them if it got out. In other words, I want you to tell me their secrets."

"...What do you mean?" Kushida still had a smile on her face, but it no longer reached her eyes.

"You said it yourself before, didn't you? That you already have enough information to bring a whole class to ruin. And you didn't just mean our own class either. You have information on the other classes too."

Kushida always worked hard to keep up appearances as a popular person, a person of strong character. People told her all kinds of things, all the time. She might not have quite as much information about the other classes as she did about Class C, but I was betting she knew something useful.

"And why do you want to know something like that, Ayanokouji-kun?" she asked.

"Do you know that Ichinose is suffering because of some rumors doing the rounds right now?"

"Yes, I know about that. There were those awful letters that went out today too..."

"I'm doing this for the sake of putting a stop to it," I told her.

"Hm. I don't really understand. Is that really *your* intention, Ayanokouji-kun? Or is it—"

"It has nothing to do with Horikita."

"Hm? Wow, you're quite compassionate then, Ayanokouji-kun. You did save Sudou-kun back then too, I suppose." Naturally, Kushida knew about the actions I had taken in order to prevent Sudou's expulsion shortly after we started school here. "So you're saying that knowing other people's personal information is somehow related to stopping the rumors?"

"Yes."

"I don't understand. If you start rumors that'll hurt more people, won't the situation just get worse? Or are you saying that that's okay, as long as it diverts attention from Ichinose-san?"

She might have assumed my strategy was to save one person by sacrificing many others. While it was certainly a logical strategy, she was wrong about it being what I had in mind.

"I'm pretty close to Ichinose-san," Kushida continued. "So if there's anything that I can do to help, then I want to help. It's certainly true that I may know more secrets than the average person. But that doesn't mean I can simply reveal them to you. Especially since they were only confided in me after I promised I wouldn't share them."

Another natural response. You'd be hard-pressed to find someone who'd react well to having their closely guarded secrets made public. One might think it was safest to simply not tell anyone your secrets at all, but human beings weren't that simple. Everyone laid bare their secrets to their families, to close friends, to lovers. Everyone wanted to share their feelings with another.

"I can't do anything to betray my friends. Besides, even if I do cooperate with you for Ichinose-san's sake, wouldn't I get found out as the person who spread the rumors?" she asked.

"We'd have to take precautions to make sure that doesn't happen, of course."

We couldn't use secrets that were so serious that they'd *only* been confided in Kushida. Conversely, secrets so trivial as to be shared with all of someone's friends didn't work either. We needed to pick secrets that were the perfect balance of known by some people, but not very many.

"Do you really think I'll help you enact a plan that I don't entirely understand? One that asks me to betray my friends like that?" she asked.

"Convincing you won't be easy, I suppose."

If I didn't know about Kushida's hidden side, then our negotiations would be dead in the water. There was no way that Kushida, who went to such trouble to play the part of an angel, would help do something that would throw others into turmoil.

But I *did* know about her true, hidden nature. Which meant we had room to talk.

"If you give me adequate information, I'm prepared to compensate you appropriately," I said.

"Compensate?"

"I intend to work on giving you what you wish for, Kushida, to the best of my ability."

"So you're saying that you'll get me what I want?"

"Yes, in a manner of speaking. That's exactly what I'll do."

"There's no guarantee that you'll keep your word. You're Horikita-san's ally, Ayanokouji-kun."

"Then consider this conversation your insurance."

"What do you mean?"

"You know what I mean. You don't need me to actually come out and say it, do you?" I briefly lowered my gaze, shooting a glance at Kushida's pocket.

"Hm?"

She was still playing dumb, so I decided to push a step further. "Even if I don't say it out loud, you should understand what I mean. A cell phone or a voice recorder. Or maybe both?"

"So, you knew, huh? That I've been recording this."

"I thought you'd at least do that much to buy yourself some insurance." It was a given that she'd try to make use of our conversation. "I mean, I expected as much from you, Kushida."

"But you were absolutely certain of it, weren't you?" She was still trying to talk her way out of it, probably because she thought I was trying to bait her into something.

"A recording would significantly lose credibility if you cut it up to remove the parts that are inconvenient to you," I said. "You'd want to use the data in its unedited form if possible. And to be able to do that, you have to be cautious with what you say and do."

Since coming to my room today, Kushida had been carefully choosing her words to be as polite as possible. She was making sure there were no faults in her behavior during our conversation, just in case something did happen.

"Hm, for you to be so sure of it from just that... Not bad."

Kushida took out her cell phone and showed me the screen to prove that she'd stopped recording.

"Okay. I'm finished recording. Ugh, that was so uncomfortable," she said. The graceful, mild-mannered vibe she'd been giving off had completely vanished. "Well, you may have expected as much, coming from me, but I knew that you were the one helping Horikita-san after all."

"I admit that I gave Horikita some ideas."

"Well, whatever, it's no big deal. I can always ask you about that in the future," said Kushida, getting to the crux of the matter. "So, how do you plan to use other people's personal information to stop the rumors about Ichinose-san?"

She leaned in forward, intent on hearing what I had to say.

"By getting the school, which has been quietly monitoring the situation, involved."

"Getting the school involved...?"

"As of this moment, Ichinose has taken no action regarding the rumors. So, naturally, the school hasn't done anything either."

"Is it safe to assume that, though? That the school will take action for Ichinose-san's sake?"

"In a manner of speaking, yes. Even if the homeroom teacher heard about what was going on, the reason nothing is being done is because Ichinose herself has yet to request the school's help. Which is why we need to escalate the situation to the point where the school can no longer ignore it."

No matter how isolated you were from the rest of the world, the world was no longer a place where information could be simply swept under the rug. If this school became a place where rumors and defamation ran rampant, which in turn led to students dropping out—or, in the worst-case scenario, committing suicide—then its status and prestige would be reduced to ruins.

The school wouldn't let something that could escalate into full-fledged bullying go unchecked. Naturally,

Sakayanagi was keeping her tactics just barely on the acceptable side of the line. In that case, I would go behind her back and push her over the line. By doing so, I would force matters to come to a head, and to eventually die down.

That was my goal.

"Not everyone is capable of remaining silent, like Ichinose-san has. So they'll go crying to the school. Is that what you're saying?"

"Yep. And even if no one does go to the school, the year-end exams are coming up. That, coupled with these rumors going around, should create a tense atmosphere. There might be arguments, perhaps even almost fights."

"And when that happens, the school will be forced to take action... Right?"

We'd disperse information that contained a mixture of truth and lies about a few students from each class. Most likely, more than half of the students targeted by the rumors would claim that they're just lies. Perhaps even all of them would refuse to admit to anything. However, the fact that some of the rumors contained elements of truth would naturally be exposed.

"If more rumors crop up right now, Class A will be the first to come under suspicion. That works to our advantage."

Sakayanagi's faction, who'd started spreading rumors to mess with Ichinose, would realize these new ones were coming from a third party. But even if they noticed, it's not like they could do anything about it. Try as they might to deny that they had anything to do with the new rumors, they couldn't deny the fact that they'd helped spread the rumors about Ichinose. As long as that remained true, there was no avoiding the fact that people would suspect them before anyone else.

Now that Kushida realized how things might go, she seemed to have figured out my plan. "But how are you going to spread so many rumors? That won't be easy."

"How? We'll use the school bulletin boards."

"Wait, bulletin boards? You mean the ones in the school app? You know that no one uses those, right? And besides, if the school does take action, won't they also punish the person who posted the rumors? Even if you can post anonymously on the bulletin boards, won't the school immediately be able to track down who the posts came from?" She peppered me with question after question.

"Naturally, I've already taken those risks into consideration."

"You're saying you're prepared for what might happen in the worst-case scenario, Ayanokouji-kun? That you might be found out?"

"Yes. And of course, if that does happen, then I won't say a word about your involvement."

I already had countermeasures in mind, of course, but I couldn't say anything was certain at this stage. Regardless, I had no intention of posting anything on the bulletin boards that could point back to me.

"This still poses a danger to me," said Kushida.

"I suppose that's true. It would be completely unnatural for me to know so much about other people's private affairs. If this did get traced back to me, people might think I'd gotten information from someone else," I replied.

It was important that I didn't handle myself *too* perfectly before Kushida. I needed to make her think there were some things I'd missed.

"So, for our own safety, we need to be extremely selective about what the rumors say."

"...Okay. I understand what your goal is, Ayanokouji-kun. I'll consider cooperating with you."

In other words, she hadn't yet decided if she actually would.

"So you're saying you'll cooperate if I accept your terms then. Is that it?"

"That's exactly it."

It would be difficult to execute this strategy without Kushida. I could easily come up with a bunch of lies, but that wouldn't be enough to really get under people's skin. It would be precisely the fact that the rumors had truth woven in with the lies that would cause people to panic. And that panic, like fire, would spread.

"Okay, then, what are your conditions?" I asked. If they were unacceptable, then our negotiations would break down.

"Horikita Suzune's expulsion."

"Unacceptable."

"I suppose so, hm?" That was Kushida's dearest wish. She knew I wouldn't grant it, but she'd asked anyway, just in case. "I suppose that asking for you to drop out would be unacceptable too, Ayanokouji-kun?"

"That would be even more unacceptable than having Horikita expelled."

"Ah ha ha." Kushida must have found my answers somewhat amusing, because she laughed out loud. "But there isn't anything else that I want."

"In that case, can I make a suggestion?" I decided to make her an offer myself.

"All right. What?"

"I'll give you half. Half of all of the private points I get moving forward."

"Wait, what? That sounds like the deal that Ryuuen made..."

Of course she already knew about the details of Ryuuen's agreement with Class A.

"Yes, it's pretty much the same thing. Of course, I'll share my statements with you if necessary, showing all my deposits and withdrawals each month so you can be sure I'm not shorting you. This will result in you getting hundreds of thousands or even millions of points by the time you reach graduation. This is an exceptional price for the information you'd be giving me."

There was a brief silence. Kushida considered it.

"It's certainly not a bad offer, I suppose. But unfortunately, I'm not really hurting for private points. It's certainly better to have more money than none, but I'm fine where I am now."

Kushida had obtained a large sum of money during the exam on the cruise ship. Even if she had spent those points lavishly, I imagined she still had quite the nest egg remaining. Still, in the end, the clearest and most effective way to negotiate was with money.

"You might have more than enough points to use for spending money, but it's never a bad thing to have more tucked away for an emergency," I said. "Chabashira-sensei said as much too, I believe. That private points may become necessary in order to protect yourself."

If you thought of it as your very own insurance policy,

then it was wise to hold onto as many points as you could, even if it wasn't much.

"No matter how I look at this proposal of yours, it looks like you're putting yourself at a disadvantage, Ayanokouji-kun. If you said that you were in danger of being expelled from school, I could understand, I suppose. But the idea that you're basically willing to give up half of your own soul in order to save Ichinose-san sounds weird to me."

"I like Ichinose."

"Spare me the jokes."

I'd thought she might laugh, but apparently, she didn't find it funny.

"I'll tell you the truth," I said. "Yes, it'll certainly hurt for me to lose out on half of my private points. But by doing so, I'll be able to protect myself."

"What are you saying?" she asked.

"I'm one of the people that you want to get expelled. There's no telling when you'll stab me in the back. In other words, this is my defense plan."

"You're saying that if you're supplying me with your private points, then you'll be a valuable resource to me, Ayanokouji-kun? Is that it?"

"Yes. Having you for an enemy is trouble I don't need. I think it's worth giving you half my points to avoid that."

The offer of private points would cement this arrangement. As long as neither one of us abandoned the other, she would continue to gain private points, which wasn't a bad deal at all.

"...I see."

After thinking it over, Kushida came to a conclusion.

"All right. I'll go along with your plan. But does that mean you're okay with the precise condition that I not do anything to antagonize you, Ayanokouji-kun, and *only* you? Don't you want to add some kind of guarantee that includes Horikita-san too?" she asked.

"I'm not that greedy. Besides, it would be more trouble for me if our agreement fell apart because I tried to protect Horikita too."

"These are extremely good conditions for me."

"If you're not comfortable with a verbal agreement, how about we put this in writing?" I asked.

"No, that won't be necessary," said Kushida, removing something from her pocket.

It wasn't a phone this time, but a voice recorder. Apparently, she hadn't just been recording on her phone; she had a backup running as well.

"I have all the evidence I need here. If you ever betray me, in any way, shape, or form... You understand what'll happen, yes?"

"Yep."

If I broke our agreement, in the worst-case scenario, she'd talk to the school. She could then bleed me dry without anyone being the wiser.

"You're really something, Ayanokouji-kun. You're completely different from Horikita-san."

Give and take. You couldn't ask someone to trust you based on emotion alone. Emotions were intangible, but numbers were concrete.

Horikita's way of doing things wasn't *wrong*. A relationship built on emotion could sometimes be stronger than one built on numbers and agreements. In this instance, however, such an approach would be a hard sell. I could have tried to persuade Kushida to swallow her feelings of resentment, but that would've been a mistake.

"Are you really okay with giving me half your points?"

"I didn't think a smaller share would really entice you."

Of course, it would be a real drain on my resources to keep paying up private points.

...But I was sure that problem would be cleared up before long.

"Well, now that we're both on the same page, can you tell me what I want to know?" I asked.

"Sure. What do you want to know?"

"Misdeeds or embarrassing stories from people's pasts

would be fine. Basically, anything that would discomfit them if it was made public."

"I see... Well, I'll tell you some things, then."

Kushida, seemingly amused by the situation, started to give me the secrets that she had been holding onto. She started by telling me things like who people were crushing on, or who they didn't like, then moved onto information about students' family situations or their histories of juvenile delinquency.

Her voice was enthusiastic and engaged. We'd made it to this stage, and she still didn't understand my true goal.

Saving Ichinose. Responding to Sakayanagi's provocation. Diverting Hashimoto's attention from me. The threat of Nagumo. All these were just components of my larger plan.

In the midst of everything going on, there was one thing I had particularly wanted to ascertain. The quantity and quality of the information that Kushida Kikyou held.

Everything I'd done was in the service of confirming that...and of getting her expelled from school.

Of course, it wasn't going to be that easy. If I went about this the wrong way, I'd be the one in trouble. I had to estimate the explosive power of the ordinance at her disposal—in other words, her overwhelming information network. And then I had to analyze that information.

Who told her these secrets? And how many other people knew them? Her grasp on the personalities and characteristics of the other students was terrifying. I could say with certainty that no one at this school held as much information as she did, at least among the first-year students.

This was Kushida's power. The ability that she had cultivated to protect herself and to make others recognize her as a shining beacon.

"I see..."

"So was that all useful?"

Of course, the information she had given me just now wasn't nearly everything that Kushida knew.

"For Class C, I want to release information about two people," I said. "Hondou and Satou."

"I guess that's fine. Satou-san's dislike of Onodera is already pretty well known." Meaning it was probably only a matter of time before Onodera found out, anyway. "I'm not the nicest person, myself...but it might be a good idea for you to remember that girls are just like that."

Kushida took out her phone and showed me her chat app. The size of my friendlist couldn't even begin to compare to hers. She was in a ton of group chats too.

"For example," she said, "look at this one chat group I made with some girls from our class. This is Group A.

You can see that there are six people in it, right? But actually, there's another group, Group B, which is made up of the same members...save one. One person has been excluded from group B. It's a girl named Nene, by the way."

Mori Nene. She was one of the girls from Kei's group of friends.

"So you're saying that people dislike Mori?"

"Exactly. If the girls post their surface feelings in Group A, then they say what they keep hidden deep down in Group B. Sometimes they'll come together in Group B and badmouth Nene. Of course, I'd never be so careless as to do something of the sort...but regardless, people might act like they get along and be all smiles on the surface, but secretly, they all have someone they don't like. It's normal for people to badmouth others behind their backs. It's not like there are only one or two examples of public and hidden groups like this. I know of dozens and dozens."

Kushida stood up, seemingly satisfied that she'd been able to talk about something she normally couldn't.

"It's late. I'm going to go back to my room now. I look forward to what comes of our agreement, Ayanokouji-kun," she said, putting on her shoes near the entrance, with her back turned to me.

"Kushida."

"Hm?"

"You've helped me a lot today."

"Oh, no, it was nothing. Well, then, goodnight, Ayanokouji-kun. I look forward to the future."

This was my chance to ask Kushida about her closeness with Nagumo. But I deliberately decided not to touch on that subject. Kushida and Nagumo coming into contact with one another was a coincidence, nothing more... which didn't mean I couldn't still use it to my advantage.

And so, using Kushida's information as my source, I began preparing "rumors" about each class to send out into the world.

8.1

FEBRUARY 14TH. Valentine's Day. That was the day I decided to deal with Hashimoto, who had been continuously tailing me during lunch and after class.

I anticipated that Kei was going to give me Valentine's Day chocolates, so I decided to take advantage of that. My guess was that she'd try to do it either early in the morning or later in the evening. There was no way she'd do it in the middle of the day, while we were at school. She'd just broken up with Hirata, and had no reason to be carrying chocolate around in her bag. Besides, even the fact that she was giving chocolates to *someone* would have caused a huge stir if it got out.

Therefore, I turned my phone off on the night before Valentine's Day. There was no chance we'd casually run into each other, but I turned it off anyway, just so I wouldn't have to come up with excuses for why it wasn't convenient to meet up in the morning. When we did meet, it had to feel natural.

Hashimoto had to be feeling pretty impatient by this point, since he had yet to see any significant results from tailing me. Which was exactly why I decided to give him a hint that something was going to happen. And what happened was Kei and I having our secret meeting, and me accepting chocolate from her.

The reason I settled on meeting with her at five o'clock was because Hashimoto had been tailing me until around six. Sure enough, he was watching the surveillance cameras in the lobby to see what I did. This was the first inexplicable opportunity he'd seen since he started tailing me, and so he boldly approached and talked directly to the two of us. Well, the results would've been much the same even if he'd just stayed back and watched.

Hashimoto was satisfied by the answer that Kei might have been the person that I was in frequent contact with. The next day, he stopped tailing me. He'd shifted his attention to preparing for the year-end exam.

And so, that was the day that I was able to move about freely.

I headed to the school building with the Valentine's chocolates I'd received from Kei still in my bag. Then, I met up with Shiina Hiyori in the library. The majority of our conversation consisted of talking about silly books, but I had an ulterior motive. Our conversation was just a lead-up to the countless rumors I planned to start circulating the next day.

I had decided to plant the seeds of the idea that Class A might be up to more than just starting rumors about Ichinose. Those seeds began to bloom a few days later. I'd deliberately chosen Ishizaki and Ibuki, both volatile and combative people, as targets of the rumors because I knew they might fly off the handle.

That was just a bonus, though. Even if the situation never deteriorated into violence, it wouldn't have made a difference in the end. What *really* mattered was when and how those messages were going to be posted on the bulletin boards.

I got in touch with the person I'd selected to solve that problem for me. Vice President Kiriyama. A student from second-year Class B who was working toward Nagumo's downfall.

After I was done talking to Hiyori in the library, I met with Kiriyama at the school building, at a time when there weren't many people around anymore. I revealed my entire plan to him. My strategy to save Ichinose.

"I see. So you're asking me to post the rumors using

my own phone? I have absolutely nothing to gain from doing that."

"That's not true. You stand to benefit from acting as my intermediary in this, Vice President Kiriyama. You see, this establishes a relationship between you and me. If I keep waiting for you to take action, that relationship would never progress."

In fact, Kiriyama had yet to instruct me to do a single thing since we had met.

"That's only to be expected," he said. "I still have my fair share of doubts about your abilities."

"I understand. Which is exactly why, rather than thinking of this as me asking for help, I'm asking you to think of it as me owing you a favor. In the unlikely event that things go bad, this will make it easier for you to rely on me. Besides, posting on the bulletin boards wouldn't be all bad for you, Vice President Kiriyama."

"...What do you mean?"

"Ichinose Honami is a valuable addition to the student council. It would be a shame to lose her. If we can get the school involved by spreading rumors on the bulletin boards, that will help protect her."

"But, if I post these rumors about the first-years, it could lead to people calling the credibility of the student council into question."

"And why is that a bad thing?"

"What...?"

"If the student council loses credibility, it hurts President Nagumo more than anyone else. If you wish for his downfall, then I think you should welcome that idea with open arms."

"That's ridiculous. It would be *real* bad for me if the school discovers I was the one who posted the rumors on the bulletin boards. Not only they would punish me, but there's also the possibility that Nagumo would relieve me of my position as vice pres—"

"You're capable of taking enough evasive measures to avoid that happening, aren't you? Honestly. I mean, you *are* going up against President Nagumo, aren't you? Or perhaps you don't have what it takes to oppose him?"

"What would a first-year like you know...?!" Kiriyama glared at me, his eyes full of anger.

"According to information I've gotten from the former student council president, President Nagumo has made contact with Kushida."

"How do you... Horikita-senpai really has placed a lot of trust in you, it seems."

"She's one of the most informed people in our entire school, regardless of grade level. So it's possible that this whole situation could be explained away as a strategy devised by President Nagumo, wherein he leaked information that he got from her via the posts on the bulletin boards. You could easily pass off a made-up scenario like that as what really happened."

This imaginary sequence of events slowly began to take shape. The idea that Kushida gave Nagumo the information, which he, in turn, instructed Kiriyama to use in order to save Ichinose.

"...You thought that far ahead about this before contacting me?" Kiriyama thought it over, probably imagining what might happen if he posted these rumors on the bulletin boards. But judging from how the conversation had gone so far, he wasn't ready to cooperate yet.

"If you say no to me here, I'll have to conclude that it means you've yielded to Nagumo. Or perhaps... I'll go ahead and report to the former student council president that Nagumo's already won you over to his side?"

What I said could have been interpreted as a threat, but it was the deciding factor in getting Kiriyama to cooperate with me.

"So will you do this for me?" I asked.

"...When should I post them?"

"Right here and now. Immediately."

If I carelessly gave him time to delay, there was a risk he might post the message using someone else's phone.

I wouldn't necessarily mind it if he did that, of course, but I wanted to avoid any chance, no matter how minute, of my plans going awry later. More importantly, I needed to keep in mind the possibility that Kiriyama might leak the information to a third party too.

"All right. But you're going to owe me a big one for this."

"Thank you very much."

I showed Kiriyama my phone screen, which displayed the rumors I'd prepared for each class. I then had him write them all down by hand. After about ten minutes of work, the entire process had been completed. I doubted any students would notice the posts right away, but I'd make sure they'd be the talk of the town tomorrow.

8.2

AND SO, the groundwork had been laid. All that remained were the finishing touches to my plans. Crushing Ichinose Honami's spirit was the last item on my to-do list...since I knew Sakayanagi would crush it herself before long, anyway.

Sakayanagi's scheme had succeeded beautifully. Ichinose continued to be absent from class even after it was thought she had recovered from her illness. It was February 18th the day that Class A and Class D clashed. It had been five days since she had gotten sick, and Ichinose still wasn't coming to class.

I was sure she'd physically recovered, but the same might not be true of her emotional scars. Knowing she was absent from class yet again, I decided to get in touch with her. But if I tried to go see her after class or during a day off, chances were high that someone would spot me. Instead, I opted to visit her on a weekday afternoon, when nearly all the dorms were empty.

I didn't contact her by phone ahead of time. I didn't plan on giving her a way out. I just showed up at her door and rang the doorbell.

"Hey, I want to talk to you a bit. Can you come out?" I asked.

A little while after, a response came from inside the room.

"I'm sorry, Ayanokouji-kun. I'm sorry to turn you away since you came out of your way to visit me, but could you please come back some time later?" she replied.

Judging by the sound of her voice, she was still in low spirits. But it seemed safe to assume that she'd completely recovered from her cold by now.

"Were those letters really such a big deal to you, Ichinose?" I asked. She didn't respond.

I sat down, leaning back against her door.

"Will you be coming to class on Monday?" I asked.

"...I'm sorry. I don't know."

It seemed like she was willing to answer questions that didn't touch on the heart of the matter, for now.

"I have some time until lunch break is over," I said. "So I think I'll hang out here for a little bit."

I just proceeded to sit quietly there until the last possible minute before lunch break ended.

"All right," I said. "Guess I'll be heading back to class."

"I...just want a little more time is all. When I'm feeling a little more put together, then I'll definitely be coming back to class. So please don't come here anymore, okay...?" I heard Ichinose say in a strained voice.

I returned to class.

8.3

THE WEEKEND HAD PASSED, and it was now the 21st. It was now Monday, and the year-end exams would start on Friday, but Ichinose was still nowhere to be seen. Kanzaki, Shibata, and some other girls who Ichinose was close to were trying to call, text, and email her, doing everything in their power to get in contact. But I didn't see them showing up at Ichinose's room after class, which I could only assume was because Ichinose had asked them not to come anymore, just like she'd asked me.

During lunch break, I slipped out of the school building and went over to Ichinose's room. I knocked lightly on her door and called out to her without waiting for an answer.

"I heard you're taking today off too?" I asked.

It was a reckless move on my part. She had told me not to come anymore, and I was ignoring her wishes.

This time, Ichinose didn't say anything back to me from the other side of the door. I didn't say anything to her either. I just sat in front of her door until the last possible minute, just like I had done the previous week.

8.4

THE SAME THING HAPPENED on Tuesday too. After confirming that she was absent from class once more, I went to Ichinose's room. I don't need to reiterate it all again.

If I were one of her classmates, she wouldn't have been able to bring herself to be really mad at me. But I wasn't. And yet, it was precisely because I belonged to another class that it wouldn't inconvenience me that much if Ichinose decided to cut all ties with me. That was the main reason why I was being so assertive.

There wasn't much time left until the year-end exam. If things continued this way, it was possible that Ichinose might be absent even on the day of the exam. Well, even if she did show up to class that day, the students of Class B were currently undergoing a great deal of mental anguish.

It was possible that their test scores would be negatively impacted by these unforeseen troubles. Even if no one wound up expelled, it would still have a big impact on their class points.

Ichinose needed to come to class on Thursday, and the students of Class B needed to feel reassured. The window in which that could be made to happen would end the next day, Wednesday.

8.5

THE END OF THAT WINDOW approached in a flash. Before I knew it, it was Wednesday.

I held a can of coffee that I bought from the convenience store in my hand. I let out a sigh, my breath visible in the air.

I wasn't going to press Ichinose that day, even though we were out of time. Because there was no way Ichinose, herself, didn't understand that today was her last chance. She would definitely take action. I was sure of it.

"February's already almost over. If we can get through the special exam next month, we'll have officially made it to our second year. They say, 'once on shore, we pray no more,' but I have to wonder if there's really any truth to that," I said aloud.

The Uninhabited Island Exam. The Cruise Ship Exam.

Paper Shuffle. Time and time again, we'd been subjected to a series of bizarre exams.

"Once we're second-year students, I wonder if the special exams will get even stranger than they are now?" I added.

"...Hey. Can I... ask you something kind of strange...?" asked Ichinose, mumbling in a quiet voice, as if she were talking to herself. It was the first time in a while she'd responded to me.

"Sure. As long as you're okay with talking to me through the door, you can ask me anything," I replied, welcoming her with open arms. But she didn't respond immediately.

"Why haven't you said anything to me, Ayanokouji-kun? Asked me anything?"

"Like what?"

"My classmates and my friends from other classes have all come by, trying to convince me to come back to school. They all say they want me to talk to them about anything that might be bothering me. And yet, Ayanokouji-kun, you've been coming here every single day without saying anything like that at all... Why?"

She probably didn't want me to worry about her, just as she hoped the other students wouldn't. She couldn't understand why I was slipping away from school every day and wasting my lunch break just to come here.

"Well, that's because those other students are really, really worried about you, Ichinose. Their attempts to convince you, again and again...that's something I could never do. My ability to connect with other people is so limited that if I tried to use my emotions to appeal to your emotions, I can't imagine it would really resonate."

I heard the faint sound of footsteps within her room. I had a feeling she was sitting on the other side of the door now. The door was the only thing separating us.

"Maybe I've been coming here every day because I'm waiting for you to just unload everything and tell me," I said.

"Waiting for me... to unload everything and tell you?"

I decided to break down the walls of Ichinose's heart for the first time.

"I know what crime you committed."

"...!"

"Well, I say that, but I don't actually know the background details or anything. But the fact that Sakayanagi dug so deeply into this, and spread it around so much that it's caused you to take time off from school, tells me how much this is weighing on you, Ichinose. But I guess there's no point in me saying that to you."

"How...do you know that?"

"That's not really important right now. I don't intend to get any deeper into it."

If Ichinose didn't want to talk about it, then our conversation would be over right here and now.

"You're probably not very good at opening up to other people about your own troubles, Ichinose. Even though you can save others, you can't save yourself. That's the kind of person you are. That's why I'm here now."

The feelings I wanted to convey had to be reaching Ichinose, little by little.

There was a brief silence. It was hard, wanting to let your emotions out, but having no one you could let them out *to*. I'd seen countless children suffer through the same thing back in the White Room. Eventually, they broke down and disappeared. Became broken people with no hope of ever recovering.

"I'm your door right now. I can't see your face and I can't reach out and touch you. I'm just a door. No one will laugh at you if you reveal your weakness to a door."

There was a light *clack* as I set my coffee down on the ground.

"So what are you going to do, Ichinose? This moment, right now, is your moment of truth."

All of Ichinose Honami's friends were reserved, gentle people. It wasn't hard to imagine them offering a deluge of kind words to their dependable leader. However, that wasn't going to work. It might seem like the correct approach to the people supporting Ichinose, but you couldn't handle this situation like it was a problem to be fixed. You just had to apply enough pressure to make her crack.

"Even someone so pathetic like me... Can I really...?"

"Who has the right to deny you that?" I asked.

"Can a criminal like me...ever really be forgiven...?"

"Everyone has the right to be forgiven."

I'd knocked on the door to her heart. All that was left now was to see how Ichinose would respond.

From the other side of the door, Ichinose slowly opened her mouth to speak.

"I... I shoplifted. And then I missed out on half a year of school during my third-year of junior high, because I was in so much pain. I couldn't talk to anyone about it. I just kept blaming myself. I holed up in a small room, just like I'm doing now..."

Ichinose started speaking, finally pulling her hands away from the wound on her heart that she'd been so desperately trying to cover for so long. She talked about what she had done. About her weakness, about how she'd retreated inward and hid herself away.

About how she told this story to Nagumo, and only him. About how Sakayanagi had approached her, asking for advice on a classmate, and told her that there was a shoplifter at our school. Ichinose had known then that it couldn't be a coincidence. She'd known Sakayanagi had probably found out about her past because she heard it from Nagumo. With no room to lie about it, all she could do was confess it all.

Ichinose had been putting on a brave face, unable to let herself be weak. Do you know how hard and scary it is to admit to your own crimes? Many immature young people have shoplifted... No, have committed *some* kind of "crime" at least once in their lives. But if you said that to a large crowd of people, they'd all probably say something like "I'd never do such a thing."

And that was only natural. Admitting to your own crimes was terrifying, as was talking about them in public. Our society is one that deals out harsh punishments in the name of justice, after all. Such is the tragic fate of a criminal. That's why they hide. That's why they never speak of their crimes, burying them deep within themselves instead. That's why they try to live on under the guise of being good people.

Ichinose, overcome by her guilty conscience, spent half a year completely alone. And then, finally, she was released from her shackles...no, she broke free of them. But her guilt would continue to follow her, no matter where she went. It would be with her until the day she died.

In fact, her guilty conscience was standing in her way right now, attacking her heart. Which was why she had no choice but to confront it.

By the time she was done telling me her whole story, lunch break was already over, but that didn't matter. Even though afternoon classes had already started, I just sat there and listened to what Ichinose had to say, without trying to console her or reprimand her.

Ichinose was softly crying on the other side of the door, trying to hold back her tears. I offered her no words of comfort, because that would have been meaningless right now. It had been clear from the very beginning who her real opponent in this battle was: herself.

It all came down to whether or not she could put an end to this herself by coming to terms with what she'd done. Very, very few people are capable of honestly facing their crimes in the true sense of the word. But when we do face our crimes...then we're able to grow and take one step forward.

And that was the conversation Ichinose and I had, before she opened up and told her friends about everything she was going through. Everything.

9   RETURN

At long last, the day of the year-end exam had come. We'd each done what we could to prepare, based on the practice test we had taken. According to Horikita, Sudou, Ike, and Yamauchi were all expected to perform quite well. Apparently, they'd done everything possible to cram during the week before the test.

Then there was Akito, Haruka, Airi, and Kei. The students in my group had all done quite well at raising their personal bars. The other students, meanwhile, had been getting help from Hirata. There were no signs of any students really struggling, so as long as everyone made sure to keep an eye on their health, the whole class should make it through this exam just fine.

Just then, I heard the sound of footsteps. Someone

was hurrying up behind me, trying to catch up, and then slowing down to match my pace.

"Good morning, Ayanokouji-kun!" Ichinose approached me, a broad smile on her face.

"Good morning, Ichinose."

"Today's finally the day, huh? The year-end exam. Did you study hard?"

"More or less, yeah. But I guess... I don't even need to ask, in your case."

I didn't even need to think about it. Class B was far more coordinated than our class, and I was sure they'd were much better prepared for the test. Even Ichinose, who'd been absent until just the other day, probably had nothing to worry about as far as academics.

"You were really cool yesterday, Ichinose. Cool enough to charm even a guy like me," I told her.

"R-really...? I suppose it's just like Sakayanagi-san said, though... that was just me being shameless."

Ichinose hadn't *really* committed a crime in the first place, though. Everything had been resolved after her mother took appropriate measures to handle it. It was a non-issue. She'd been carrying a completely unnecessary burden. Nothing more.

"It's all thanks to you that I was able to get back on my feet, Ayanokouji-kun."

"I can't be a shoulder to lean on and worry about you like the students of Class B can, though. I just thought I'd try to listen, is all. It's nothing you need to thank me for."

"No, that's not true... If you weren't there, Ayanokouji-kun, I think I would definitely have ended up self-destructing and falling apart, just like last time. In that sense, Sakayanagi-san completely defeated me this time."

Sakayanagi had manipulated Ichinose with devastating success, driving her to the brink of self-destruction. It was certainly true there was no telling what would have happened had I not gotten involved. But I wanted to make something clear.

"I don't want you to feel like you owe me too much, though. I was nothing more than the catalyst. In the end, you're the only one who was able to overcome your own past," I told her.

"...Yeah, I suppose you're right. I can't ever undo what I did. No matter how much time passes, there may never come a day where I feel like my sins have truly disappeared. But...from this point onward, I can face life head-on. I'm sure of it."

Everything should be all right now. No matter who tried to blame her, Ichinose would be able to stand her ground. She'd grown strong—stronger than anyone else.

I expected she'd grow into an even more formidable rival in the future.

Even so, there were no guarantees in life.

"If you're ever feeling like you're about to lose sight of yourself, you can talk to me again."

"Huh...?"

"When that time comes... Yeah. I should be able to at least listen."

Ichinose stopped and stood completely still. "Is it okay for me to depend on you...?" she asked.

"If you're okay with someone like me."

"Really?" she asked again.

"...Yeah, really." I nodded, though I was somewhat confused by the question.

"...Th-thank you..." she said quietly. A rather unusual reaction from Ichinose, who was usually so upbeat.

Then she quickly shook her head, maybe because she, too, realized her reaction had been out-of-character.

"B-but... won't you come to regret it someday?" she asked, gazing deeply at me.

"Hm, I guess you've got a point. I mean, our class might get stuck in B. If you and your class graduate from A, then my classmates might end up blaming me for it."

"R-right?" she answered, scratching her cheek with a wry smile.

"Well, if that time comes, just don't tell Horikita."

"...heh heh. Yeah, okay. I'll make sure to do that."

Ichinose, walking alongside me once more, stretched her shoulders. She looked bright and cheery again, as if she'd just been reborn. Well, then. All that remained was to get through the year-end exam.

She was still quietly looking over at me.

"What is it?" I asked.

"H-huh?"

"You've been staring at me for a while now. If there's something you want to say, I'm all ears."

"Well, to tell you the truth, I... Ah! Sorry, Ayanokouji-kun. Can you please wait a little bit?"

Just as Ichinose was about to say something, her attention shifted to another student in front of us. A brief glance in the direction of that student, and the people surrounding them, made it obvious what was up.

"I'm sorry. I'm going to head over there for just a sec," said Ichinose, leaving my side and running to catch up to the student in front of us. "Good morning, Nagumo-senpai."

"Oh, Honami. You're looking cheerful this morning." Nagumo might have been surprised by the sight of Ichinose's restored smile.

"Because that's just the way I am."

"Don't you resent me, Honami?" he asked.

"Resent you?" replied Ichinose, tilting her head to the side in apparent confusion.

Immediately afterward, though, she seemed to understand the meaning behind his question.

"I don't resent you at all, Nagumo-senpai. All I am is grateful to you. Really, thank you so much for bringing me onto the student council. I'll do my best from here on out, so I'm looking forward to working with you."

"I see. Well, it would seem like you're going to exceed my expectations."

Nagumo looked over at me for just an instant, then immediately turned around and walked away.

It wasn't difficult to intuit what he was saying with that look. He had wanted to break Ichinose Honami down and build her back up with his own hands. He had intended to completely tame her and make her his pawn.

The look he'd just given me conveyed his displeasure that I'd thrown off his plans—which meant he understood that I'd been involved in this incident in some capacity.

Ichinose bowed to Nagumo and then came back over to me once again.

"Hey!" she called, her voice noticeably loud. She opened her mouth wide and continued speaking. "Um, hey, so, listen."

While she spoke, she reached into her school bag. Then she froze.

"What is it?" I asked.

"Umm, well, it's... Th-this is odd. It's just, well, I had planned to just be like 'Here you go!' but..."

Ichinose seemed to hesitate, still digging around inside her bag, but then seemingly made up her mind and took something out. She handed it over to me.

"This is a little bit late, but...will you accept these Valentine's chocolates from me? It's just, well, I've never given anyone chocolates like this before, and... This is the only way that I can express my gratitude, so..."

"You don't have to force yourself to pay me back by giving me something, you know?"

The 14th had already passed, but I certainly wasn't upset to be given more chocolate by a girl. That said, I hadn't done what I had for the purposes of getting chocolate from her. She didn't need to feel obligated to give me any.

"I-I-I'm not forcing myself, though! Y-you don't want it?"

"No, I do... Thank you."

The chocolates might start to melt if we stayed out too long. Not to mention people would notice us. And so, I gratefully accepted Ichinose's gift.

POSTSCRIPT

I WAS CASUALLY THINKING about the advantages of living in Tokyo the other day. You see so many restaurants in the media—I thought maybe I should go eat at one of them myself. But there's probably been more than a few occasions when a place is shown on TV, and right after, becomes so popular that you can't even get in. Even worse, the prices get way too steep...

Oh, hey there. It's been a while. It's the guy who felt like Volume 8 had only just been released yesterday, but now realizes we're already at the release of Volume 9: Kinugasa.

I just can't help but feel concerned about my health these days. Because of the nature of my occupation, I spend almost two-thirds of my day sitting down. My blood circulation is getting worse and worse and my back is hurting more. When I was young, I could push through somehow, thanks to my physical prowess. But now I can't really fake it to get by anymore. I've been going in for regular checkups and everything, but I kind of feel like... you know, as long as there's no way to really address the root of the problem, the future doesn't hold much hope.

Anyway, the story of Volume 9 focuses on Valentine's Day and the time leading up to the year-end exam. The protagonist has gradually started to become surrounded by more and more girls. I've been wondering if there's a chance that he might actually make some progress with a girl, deepen his relationship with her, in his second year of school.

The story also focused on Ichinose, who hadn't really had much time in the spotlight so far in the series. There were no special exams this time around, so the story unfolded in a relatively peaceful (?) way, but it's getting to be more serious.

Finally, the first-year arc will come to an end with the special exam featured in the next installment, Volume 10. There have been times where I've thought to myself... "They're still in their first year, even though it's been close to *four* years since the series started?" So, from here on out, things may start to develop a little bit faster...maybe. (I still don't know yet.)

The words my editor said to me at the time I started this series are still in my mind, even now.

"I'm glad that this is a work where time always moves forward."

No matter how long it takes, the end will eventually come. I laughed at first when I heard that, but now I'm convinced it's true. I have a pretty serious look on my face as I think about it now. I'm thinking I'd like to show you how the class points and the main character's private points are coming along in the next volume, if possible.

Anyway. Let's meet again in Volume 10, everyone.